The
Clinker

The
Clinker

ROGER VAUGHAN CARR

Houghton Mifflin Company
Boston 1989

Copyright © 1989 by Roger Carr
First American edition 1989
Originally published in Australia in 1989 by
Houghton Mifflin Australia Pty Ltd

Library of Congress Cataloguing-in-Publication Data:

Carr, Roger
  The Clinker / Roger Carr,—1st American ed.
    p.   cm.
    Summary: Having come from Boston to spend the summer in Australia
  with his great-grandparents, thirteen-year-old Rust is consumed with
  doubt that he can live up to the responsibilities they lay on him.
    ISBN 0-395-51737-0
    [1. Australia—Fiction. 2. Grandparents—Fiction.] I. Title.
  PZ7.C2299CL 1989
  [Fic]—dc19   89-31088
                                                                      CIP
                                                                      AC

Printed in Australia by Australian Print Group

10 9 8 7 6 5 4 3 2 1

Chapter One

"Sealers Inlet. . .?" the booking clerk repeated. "No, never heard of it, sonny." Then he saw the despair in the boy's eyes and felt sorry for him. "Where's it supposed to be?"

"On the Southern Highway."

Rust was trying not to cry. He felt so tired and disoriented and alone after the flight from Boston that he really only wanted to find a place where he could fall asleep.

"First time in Australia, eh?" the clerk said, and went on without waiting for an answer. "Relax. We'll find it for you. The route driver on the Southern will know." He turned to an open doorway. "Hey, Bill. Young American boy here was told to take a bus to Sealers Inlet. Know it?"

A man came in. "Sure." He looked at Rust. "I go through the Inlet, leaving in half an hour."

"Oh, *thank* you!" Rust's face had lit up.

The man grinned. "Don't have to thank me. It's on the route. Put your things in 36 over there, and go to sleep on a seat if you like. You look bushed."

"I've just flown from Boston."

"Ah, then you'd be old Pa Stewart's grandson."

"His great-grandson," Rust corrected eagerly, a surge of relief running through him. "You know him?"

"Sure. He pioneered that country. Fix your ticket and get some sleep. I'll take you right to the door."

Rust had meant to see every mile of roadside leading to the Inlet, but when the driver shook him awake and he sat up ready to see if the coastline really was as wonderful as Dad and Grandad had told him, he found that they were parked on a sandy track outside an old weather-board house snugged in amongst twisted trunks of tea-tree—a house he had looked at a thousand times in the photo albums back home.

"Don't think they've heard the bus. Want me to give 'em a honk?"

Rust shook his head, trying to stretch the sleep from his eyes. "I . . . I'll surprise them. We couldn't tell them exactly when to expect me. I was going to ring from the airport, but—" He shrugged.

"You didn't look like you could remember anything much back at the depot. It's a long flight."

Rust picked up his coat and travelling-bag and climbed out after the driver. "Thanks for bringing me."

Bill put the two cases down. "Enjoy yourself." He climbed back into the bus and backed it away towards the highway. A quick wave to the boy left standing by the gate, and he was gone.

Rust draped his coat across one of the cases and looked round, a broad smile breaking across his face as the familiar photograph came alive. The picket gate hanging open, its top hinge rusted through; the picket fence in need of hammer, nails and paint; a few flowers along the path leading to the veranda steps—the only cultivated flowers on the whole property, he knew, because in any place other than the vegetable patch the salt winds burnt them off.

And they had been weeded in the last day or two, he could see.

He felt a tingle of anticipation, but resisted the urge to rush inside and looked instead at the house itself—at the corrugated iron of the roof in its faded pink and rust-stain red; at the two brick chimneys bleached and salt-whitened on the weather side, which he could just make out, but still brick-red on the lee that was towards him.

The sea-winds! Dad and Grandad always talked of the sea-winds, the driving winds that bent everything inland. The sea-winds, and. . . He turned his head slightly to listen. Yes, the sounds of the Bass Strait boomers. He could hear them, crumping down on the beach beyond the wide waters of the Inlet and the dunes: the heartbeat of the valley.

He clenched his fists as the zinging excitement rolled back the tiredness of the journey; breathed in the salty, grassy, even muddy smells that both Dad and Grandad said they could still remember; and had to stop himself from bursting into a run right down the path beside the house to *see* it all on the other side. But his great-grandparents would want to be there when he did, would want to show him the places and things his grandfather, their son, had grown up with—and those his own father, their grandson, had known on his vacations before he had moved to America.

If only it wasn't so late in the afternoon. He needed hours and hours and hours.

He threw the coat over one shoulder, tucked the travelling-bag under one arm and hefted the two cases, then found he could not fit through the gateway and had to take the cases one at a time.

They were filled mostly with presents for his great-grandparents, including a new set of hinges and screws for the gate. He certainly hadn't brought much in the way of clothes. Dad had said shorts, T-shirts and a couple of pullovers, with three pairs of sneakers and some socks, would be just about right. Mom, of course, had thought of sensible things like underwear, and had insisted on a pair of jeans.

And don't use the front door, he suddenly remembered her saying as he put his foot on the step. *No one in country Australia ever uses a front door.*

He altered direction and pushed the cases through the encroaching grasses and tea-tree along the track that ran round the side of the house, and there it was!—a sliver of the Inlet through the trees. Just like he had always been told, just like in the photos; a silver splinter of what he knew was a great sheet of water with dunes on the other side. He had to force himself to go on. This was the water where his father and grandfather had adventured when they were boys. The water where the *Clinker*—

He made himself stop thinking, dreaming, and went on round to the back door under its corrugated-iron lean-to shelter. He set the cases down to knock.

"Come in," a deep old voice called.

Rust turned the handle and pushed the door open across the scrape on the ancient lino, lifted his cases into the small entrance-room, and pushed the door closed behind him.

"That you, Bob? Maggie an' Ma have gone down t' pick some strawberries."

Rust left his things and went through the next door to the kitchen, and then stopped. His great-grandfather was seated in front of the open fire-door of the wood stove, an old, old man; a great, tall man with huge hands but a shrunken, bony body too small for the suit-coat he was wearing. His head turned towards Rust, puzzled.

"G'day. You one of th' youngsters from th' new holiday houses?" And then, before Rust could answer, the old man pushed himself to his feet, his eyes wide, crazy-looking, Rust thought—until he saw the effort at a smile, and then the tears: large, full, glistening tears that sprang and rolled from the deep sockets of the eyes as the old man stepped across to him and the great bony hands reached out and grasped his shoulders.

"Russell? By God, it *is* you! Welcome home, son." And before Rust could answer he was enfolded in the long arms, pressed into the musty coat till he could hardly breathe.

"Nell! Nellie!" the old man roared, then held Rust out

at arms' length—and the tears welled and rolled and welled again from his eyes and he was unable to speak. He could only smile, shake his head, grip the shoulders of the boy more tightly.

"I should have rung you from the airport, Pa."

Pa shook his head, and the movement said *It doesn't matter*.

"The busdriver brought me right to the front gate." Rust could not think of anything else to say. "I went to sleep as soon as I was on the bus and didn't wake up till we were stopped outside."

"By God," Pa managed. "Ma. . . !"

The outer door burst open and a girl, a little younger than Rust—Maggie, he guessed—ran in, eyes wide with urgency. "She's coming, Pa! We heard you from—" She stopped, and her eyes flashed briefly with . . . Rust could not be sure, but he saw the sudden curl of her lip, and then she was gone, sandy hair and bare legs like an out-of-focus picture.

"Maggie?" he asked.

Pa snorted confirmation. "Shy as a brushtail. *Ma!*"

"Coming, coming. What *is* it?" The old lady stumbled in, face flushed, expecting some terrible calamity.

"It's our boy. He's here."

"Russell . . ." she whispered. "What a foolish old lady!" She brushed sudden tears from her eyes as she came towards him, then held out her arms and folded him to her. "You've come, you've really come! It's like a dream. He's really here. He really is." She turned her head towards the door. "Maggie, isn't he just like his pictures?" But there was no answer. "Must have gone back for the strawberries. We'll need extra now you're here. We'll have a celebration for the four of us for your safe coming."

"Can I run out and tell her about the extra strawberries?" Rust asked. He wanted a moment away, just long enough to fix in his mind the switch from rigid photographs and disembodied telephone voices to real living people.

"Hurry, then," Ma said. "I'll set up. Pa, get a bottle of your stone ginger."

"You're a fine-lookin' fella," Pa said, standing back with pride.

Rust smiled quickly and went. He had been looking forward to this meeting for so long, and he was not disappointed, but . . . well, somehow, just for the moment, to be hugged and cried over was more than he could cope with right away.

He stopped when he was beyond the lean-to door-shelter and looked into the tangle of the backyard. There was no sign of Maggie. His mother and father had told him to give her a special thankyou from them for the time she spent with Ma and Pa. She was always mentioned in Ma's letters, and there was a special present for her in one of the cases.

"Maggie?" he called. There was no answer, so he started along the path towards the small shed, but stopped when it forked. He studied the sand. Shoes and bare feet went to the right: that must be the fork that led to the vegetable patch, a square garden, he knew, fenced with tea-tree stakes against the winds.

He followed it down through the twisted trunks of the low trees to a gate in a thickly thatched and overgrown fence. The gate was open, and half a billy of strawberries stood just inside. He collected it, and added half-a-dozen more strawberries before he turned back.

"Maggie! Ma wants you to come in for a party."

There was still no answer, but a twig cracked and his eyes flicked to a cluster of bare toes showing in the low fork of a tree.

"Maggie!" He put the billy down and ran. But she was too quick for him, slipping out of the tree and dashing off, the soles of her feet, so white against the warm brown of her legs, looking like skipper-fish dancing on their tails across water.

"Maggie!"

She was already gone, and he stopped as he reached the edge of the brush on the banks of the Inlet, and forgot her at the sight of the wide sheening waters, and drew in a long breath of wonder. He was really here . . .

He looked across to the left, where the ruins of the old signal station sat high on the plateau, the land running up from a low cliff above a narrow beach. The beach ran out under the cliffs to widen where it met the bar, a stretch of sand that held the waters of the Inlet back from the ocean. The right-hand side of the bar met the sand-dunes that stretched away to the right for as far as he could see; and on their far side was the ocean.

On this side of the Inlet the banks were grassy tussocks and low scrub, and somewhere in front of him there would be a jetty, and . . . the *Clinker*.

"Russell . . .?" The voice was dim, remote.

He turned and ran back through the scrub, feeling guilty that he had gone as far as he had and seen so much without them. "Coming . . ."

He collected the billy and ran back to where Pa stood just outside the door-shelter, and was surprised again by the height of him. Dad had always said Pa was a giant of a man, but Rust had never imagined just how tall and how broad—even with the shrinking caused by the years.

"Been having a look around?" Pa asked, and Rust detected disappointment in his voice.

"No. I just chased after Maggie to try and get her to come in."

"Ah." Pa was satisfied. "Didn't think she would. Does her schoolin' at home. Won't even talk t' th' new people comin' down on holidays. Father's th' same way. Works alone in th' bush an' so shy he can't look you in th' eye. Two of 'em spend all their spare time in th' water on surfin' boards." He put an arm around Rust. "Mother's different." They went into the kitchen. "Maggie's gone flighty, Ma. Have t' celebrate without 'er."

Ma took the billy of strawberries, her long white hair tied up in a bun now, a few wispy hairs from her hurry protruding like tendrils of golden smoke where they caught in the shaft of late-afternoon sunlight that streamed through the window.

She had changed into a black white-spotted dress, and the apron Rust could remember Mom sending her for last Christmas.

"We'll give them a quick rinse and have them with cream."

"Think m' stone ginger might be a bit powerful for a boy, Nellie?" Pa asked. "Everyone into th' shelters while I defuse 'er!" He eased the wire catch that held the china stopper in place, and ginger-beer fizzed from the top. "Think a Yankee can handle th' hard stuff?"

"I'll try," Rust grinned.

Ma had the kitchen table set with a white cloth and silver cake-forks beside the rose-patterned bowls. "I was going to make a quick batch of scones," she said. "Then I decided the strawberries would be enough for a first celebration at this time of day. You don't want to be around the house talking before you've been out to look around."

"I've *got* to see the *Clinker*."

"Right after we've eaten," Pa promised.

"That girl's not coming back," Ma said as she put the strawberries on the table. "We'll save her some in the fridge."

"Be more sense puttin' 'em in a bowl outside th' back door like you'd feed a wildcat," Pa snorted.

Ma gave Rust a hug. "You sit there. Do you eat in the kitchen at home?"

"Sometimes."

"I think it's probably an Australian custom. I tried to

change it when we were first married, set our meals in the dining-room; but Pa was used to the kitchen."

"No sense tryin' t' have two rooms warm an' com- f'table," Pa said. "Anyway, it's company for you when you're workin'—and the only time I really got a chance t' be with you when I was on th' wood."

Ma patted the old man fondly on the hand and sat down. "Try Pa's ginger."

Rust did, and coughed. "It's strong."

Pa grunted with pleasure. "M' own recipe. Put fire in y' heart!"

"What do we call you?" Ma asked. "The letters always say *Rust*. Is that the name you like best?"

"I guess. Everyone always calls me that."

"Good name for th' coast," Pa said. "That's what everything does down 'ere, rusts, so it'll suit nicely."

"We'll show you your room, soon as we've eaten," Ma said. "It's the same room your grandfather had when he was a boy, and your own father when he came down for holidays before they went to America. I haven't made up the bed. I thought I'd wait till you got here so the sheets would be dry. Everything gets a little dampish on the coast if it's not used regularly. But it's all ready for you. Pa's rubbed up all the old things."

"An' got you a rod an' gear too," Pa added. "Fixed up an old split cane I made for your father." He frowned. "Or *his* father . . ."

"I'll clear up while you show him the room, Pa. And the bathroom. Take him in now, and then we'll all go down to the jetty and see the *Clinker*."

Pa took the two cases, and Rust the coat and bag, up the short hallway to a door.

"You open 'er up an' see if she's like you imagined."

Rust turned the handle and opened the door, slowly . . . and it *was* just as he had imagined, only there was a honey glow he had not expected, a glow that came from the chest of drawers, the bed and the wardrobe, all furniture that Pa had made himself from the wreck of the *Ohio*, which had gone to pieces on Tambourine Reef just off the point; a glow that came also from the gleaming brass of the ship's oil-lamp—which, he could see from the moist blackness of the wick, was still in use, although there was a candle on the bedside table too.

"Well?"

Rust nodded and turned and grinned, tossed the bag and coat onto the bed, and ran to the window. Tea-tree branches brushed against the glass beyond the white net curtains, and through a small opening in the leaves he could just make out the western dunes.

"Nailed that winder shut once. Had to, when your grandaddy got too adventurous and took t' sneakin' away of nights for rock fishin'. Dangerous out there for a man, an' no chance for a boy young as he was then. Eight or ten. You can still see th' nail holes."

Rust looked at the blue-black surrounds of the puttied-up holes in the bottom of the frame, and smiled. It was hard to imagine Grandad as a truant boy.

"I was pretty mad that night," Pa admitted. "An' Ma was too, when she saw th' nails! Never could get th' holes patched up quite right when I finally pulled them out. Come on, then, go an' change an' we'll get off down th' Inlet. Bathroom's straight across th' hall. Got one of them sep'ic tanks a few year back t' make it easier for your Ma. Still use th' one out back m'self."

"I'll hurry." Rust tipped a case over and dropped to his knees. Shorts and T-shirt were all he'd require; their freedom was marvellous after his travel clothes, and the coolness of boards under his hot sweaty feet was great. He wouldn't put anything back on his feet. If Maggie could go barefoot...

He crossed to the bathroom, then went back to the kitchen.

"Need something on your feet," Ma said.

"But Maggie—"

"Might be tough enough for that when y've been 'ere a week or so," Pa said.

"'K." He returned to the room and reluctantly put on socks and sneakers. Then he slid the window open, climbed out, and ran along the side of the house and round the back. Ma and Pa were already in the lean-to shelter, Ma changing into waterboots while Pa, wearing an old felt hat now, slashed a walking-stick at a creeper that intruded from the roof.

"I came out through the window."

"Have to buy some more nails, Pa."

"Buy 'em? I've still got boxes of 'em from th' old *Ohio* out in th' shed. Come on, let's get down t' th' *Clinker*."

Pa led the way along the narrow track, past the small shed and the outside privy. The track was similar to the ones that led in from the front gate to the vegetable garden: grey sand, with grasses, bushes and tea-tree growing in from the sides. Before long the tea-tree closed over the top, forming a natural canopy and making the path a tunnel until the canopy parted and the growth became more and more stunted; it ended at little more than ankle-height, a bushy wedge forced into the prevailing winds.

"By God!" Pa roared as they reached the beginning of the bank, a wide strip of tussocky grass, bare patches, pigface and low brittle plants with tiny yellow button-flowers. "What th' devil d' y' think y' doin'?" He started forward in a shaky run, and Rust saw, on the water just beyond the end of the jetty, a gleaming white-hulled boat, with two boys of fourteen or fifteen aboard it.

The *Clinker*?

"Little devils!" Ma snapped, and started after Pa as the boys, using broken planks as oars, began paddling urgently for the bank. They reached it just ahead of Pa, leapt into the shallows and took off.

"I'll skin y'!" Pa bellowed after them, waving his stick. "Catch y' near 'er again an' I'll whip y'!" He stopped at the edge of the water and hooked the boat in with the crook of his stick. "Damned holiday people." He took a deep breath and turned. "Had 'er all moored up neat so you'd see 'er at 'er best first time, son," he puffed.

"They're beginning to spoil so much," Ma said, looking at the receding boys and patting Pa on the arm. "I suppose we're lucky we got down before they were away."

"It hasn't spoilt it for me," Rust assured them quickly. "It's still . . . like a photograph come alive." He squatted down and reached out a hand to touch the vessel, as though to confirm to himself that she was real.

Four metres long with a pointed bow and flat stern; a wide rowing-seat amidships, a smaller one in the stern; bow partly decked in to add strength for the hole that took the mast; brackets for leeboards; brass plates for the thole pins of the rowlocks; brass mooring-rings on her bow-post and stern. . . Every line of her beauty—every lapped board—perfect.

"She'll be sixty-two on your grandfather's birthday," Pa said proudly, "an' not a patch of rot or a split in th' length or breadth of 'er!"

"She's beautiful, Pa."

"When he heard a child was coming he worked every night after he got in from the bush, till your grandfather was born," Ma said. "No matter how he felt after a day on the logs, he always put an hour or two into the boat. The day after your grandfather was born the three of us christened her and went out on the Inlet. The very day after."

"Well, come on! Get us a pair of oars, son."

Rust did not need to be told where they were kept—in the long lidded box at the back of the jetty by the brightly green, fleshy-leafed tree thriving in this climate that bent and stunted even the hardy tea-tree. He ran along the bank while Pa walked the *Clinker* after him.

"I've put your rod an' gear in there, too," Pa said. "Just remember, nothing goes back in th' locker without bein' wiped down."

Rust lifted the lid. Along with the three rods, in their own section, the box contained three oars, a mast and boom, leeboards, rudder and tiller, three battered life-jackets, and sails.

"Expect you'll be doin' a lot of sailing, if y' anything like y' grandfather," Pa said, watching him. "Come on. Get th' oars an' I'll show you th' back paddock."

"Back paddock?" Rust lifted out two of the oars.

"Some people have grass; we have water in ours." He leaned and worked the boat around till the stern was aground. "Hold her in nice an' tight while I get aboard."

"Did you just finish painting her, Pa?"

"Seemed as good a time as any. Gettin' a bit weather-worn, an' we didn't want you goin' back home an' sayin' th' old people weren't keepin' the *Clinker* up t' scratch."

Ma held the stern while the old man eased himself aboard. "Go on, son."

"Aren't you coming too?" Rust asked her, surprised.

"I'll get things done about the house. Plenty of time for me later."

Rust was disappointed, but he passed the oars to Pa and helped Ma push the stern off the mud as he kneeled aboard.

"We won't be so long," Pa said, fitting the rowlocks and swinging the oars out. He stroked the *Clinker* round till her head was pointing for the bar, and leaned back against the deeply dipped blades.

"Bye, Ma!"

"Take your time," she called back.

Rust settled himself in the stern seat. "She almost skims," he exclaimed, having expected a boat of this size to plough.

"These timbers have been t' th' bottom once. Don't want t' go again, son."

"You did build her from bits of the *Ohio?*"

"Yup. Dug 'em out of th' sand."

"Dug?"

"She went down in ninety-six, afore I were even born. Bits of 'er washed up an' buried right along th' beaches. Th' Tambourine was a cruel reef t' th' sailin' ships."

"Is that why they built the old signal station?"

"Nuh. That was there back in th' late seventeen-hundreds for th' sealers. Was a beacon, not a warning. They reckon th' sealers used th' Inlet as a base, an' even kept th' bar open so they could bring their boats into safe water. We'll go down th' bar now an' you can get out an' have a look at th' beach." He pulled the boat on down the wide waters, in the direction of the bar and the ocean. The sound of the rolling breakers grew louder, their wild white manes showing suddenly above the sand.

"Wow!" Rust turned to look behind, surprised by how completely the tea-tree hid the house, so that only the chimneys showed—as on the other old house where he knew Maggie lived.

"When did they build *them?*" he asked, pointing to the two modern sharp-angled homes of pink cedar and sheet glass that were not hidden at all, but rose like slashes of fluorescent graffiti across the face of an old master. "Dad and Grandad would be disappointed."

"Yeh," Pa agreed curtly. "That's why we never mentioned 'em. Holiday people. Too much time on their hands, these days. Too much money too."

Rust felt a twinge of guilt at the thought of the beach-house his parents owned back home, and he looked further back to the rolling hills of the forest of the Otway Ranges, where Pa had worked all his life felling the great red ironbarks for the mills.

"Sternman! Ready t' go ashore," Pa rumbled, and Rust got up on his knees as his great-grandfather spun the boat around in her own length and backed her onto the bar.

"Will I pull her up?" he asked, stepping out and turning to hold the stern against the sand.

"Nuh. I'll stay aboard this time. You run on over an' have a look at th' beach an' see what you think of it."

"I won't be long." He turned and galloped up the slope of the bar to the low crest and stopped, sucking in the air, perhaps trying to suck in the whole wonderful scene before him—the great rolling breakers whose thunder he could feel through his feet; the long curving beach to his right that ran away until it disappeared in a mist of distance; to his left the lumping great black rocks shouldering the incoming rollers disdainfully aside, so that by the time they reached the rocky beach below the cliffs on which the old signal station stood, they had lost their form and some of their power and could do no more than bite spitefully at the beach itself in frustration; and the Tambourine Reef, nearly a kilometre offshore, barely showing itself now at high water.

"I'm going down," he shouted back to the boat, and sprinted to the very edge of the beach where the waves ran up and thinned out until they were just a glisten on the sand, wishing he had been able to bring his surfboard over with him.

He kicked a hole with the toe of one sneaker, watched the hole fill with water that seeped out of the sand, then ran backwards to the dry and sat there and pulled his sneakers and socks off and ran again onto the wet and through the shallows, imagining other feet, Grandad's fifty years ago when he was thirteen, Dad's twenty-six years ago when he was thirteen, running *here*, like *this!*

He had the years worked out because that was all a part of the plan for this visit: to do the same things they had done when they were thirteen here.

Just out from the beach was the wide rock-table— covered now by the flood—where they had fished for the new-coin-silver sweep, the rockies, the bluenose, the leatherjacks. In the shallow scoop between the beach and the rocks—the tide would be right now—was the mullet-run where those sweet-fleshed fish *threw* themselves at the bait, Dad said.

Rust turned and ploughed across the soft sand to the base of the dunes, then dropped to all fours and clambered up between the marram-grass clumps and the round blue cushion-bushes until he was on the ridge and could look along the wide curve of the beach. There was someone surfing a few hundred metres beyond the rock ledge, and he watched him, enviously, right into the sand before turning to look inland.

From here he could see right across the Inlet and back into the ranges again, but was high enough now to take in the intervening ground as well, the flat land with its narrow strip of grazing where the river wound, wide at first but narrowing quickly to a tiny stream before it disappeared into bushland.

Down this end the valley was wider. There were green paddocks on the hillside to the right where dairy cattle instead of horseteams now grazed. That had been Pa's land, once; but he had sold it a few years ago. Other land, on the flats each side of the creek, was less green; but he still owned that, just in case—and Rust felt sad for a moment—just in case Dad, or Grandad, or even he, ever wanted to come back from America and use it.

But they never would, and that seemed awful...

He dropped his eyes and looked down to the bar. There was the *Clinker*. There was Pa. He sucked in a long, deep breath and felt as if, in one way, he was going to cry; in another, as if he was going to burst apart with the sheer excitement of it all.

"Pa...!"

Pa lifted his stick in acknowledgement and Rust plunged back down the dune, taking wild leaps out into space and landing with both feet against the sand, moving great avalanches of it until he was back on the beach, where he sprinted, trying to gather in his sneakers on the run and tumbling and rolling in the sand; laughing aloud as he crawled back for them; running again. "It's just like they said, just exactly the same!"

"Well, they used t' do th' rowin', so I guess you best do that too," Pa said. "Shove off."

Rust pushed the *Clinker* away and crawled past Pa. "Is the bar going to break while I'm here?" he asked, sitting and unshipping the oars.

"It might. The Inlet's well filled. Hoped it would be, t' give you lots of sailin' room." Pa looked thoughtfully across the wide waters, then back to the bar for a moment. "A good storm in th' hills would take 'er out, though."

"Which is best?" Rust asked, leaning back and hauling. "When it's full or when it's empty?"

"No best," Pa told him. "Full like this you've more room t' set a sail; but when she's risin' an' fallin' with th' tides, that's got its own interests. How are you as a swimmer?"

"Good. Surfing and sailing are my favourite sports."

"Well, they're th' ones t' have here. Your Ma taught your grandfather an' your father t' swim before they were allowed out of our sight. If you can swim you can take th' *Clinker* out any time you want. But don't go on th' rocks by yourself, or swimmin' in th' sea."

"I won't," Rust promised.

"See if you can make friends with Maggie; then y'll have someone t' go with." His eye caught a movement on the bar, and he turned to look more closely. "There's her dad now. Take us back t' say g'day."

Rust hesitated. He was facing astern and had seen the man before Pa, but he didn't really want to waste time talking to anyone except his great-grandparents just yet.

"Come on, swing her round."

Rust backed an oar and turned the *Clinker*'s bow back for the bar. The man changed direction to meet them, crouching to wait on the sand at the edge of the water, with his board across his knees. "Meet our great-grand-son Rust," Pa said proudly. "Rust, Mr Roberts—Maggie's dad."

"Hi," Mr Roberts said softly, his eyes not quite meeting Rust's. He was blond, like his daughter, with long hair tied back in a ponytail and a thin, wispy beard; not the kind of person Rust could imagine a man like Pa having anything to do with. He even wore an earring and a silver-mounted shark's tooth on a leather thong around his neck. But Pa sounded as though he really liked him.

"You'll have to come out and spend a day in the bush with me, Rust. To see where your Pa cut the forest giants."

"I'd like that, Mr Roberts."

"Bob," he said, and shivered.

"You get home an' into somethin' warm, young fella," Pa said. "Just wanted t' introduce you."

"Don't forget, Rust," Bob said, standing.

"Thanks."

He pushed them off. "Enjoy it."

Rust leaned forward and dipped and pulled, stretching his muscles to their utmost to get the stiffness from them, feeling excitedly alive but strangely tired. "It's probably after midnight at home," he remarked, watching the sun's last rays vanish behind the western ranges. "Even the sleep on the bus hasn't really worked."

"Imagine it'll take a while t' get used t' th' new time," Pa said. "Turn round an' have a look at th' swans up by th' swamps."

Rust rested the oars and searched the darkening waters way up past the jetty.

"Here come th' rest of th' mob." Pa pointed to the sky above the dunes. "Wait an' watch 'em in. They'll have been out fishin' th' ocean all day. Only stay around here when it's stormin'."

Rust looked where Pa was pointing with his stick and

quickly found the cluster of dark forms, high in the pale-green evening sky, heading in towards them, crossing the shore way above the bar and swinging in a wide circle around the Inlet—eight of them, flashes of white at their wingtips—before they came down, line astern, and their feet trailed and shaved silver splinters from the black water as they settled and melded amongst the ripples of their own making on the dark sheen.

"Probably th' great-great-grandsons of th' very ones your own father knew," Pa said, and gave a slight shiver as a sudden chill breeze that had come in through the gap between the dunes and the cliffs slipped up the Inlet and passed on. "Let's go on in an' get us a good fire goin'."

Rust pulled on towards the jetty, backed his oars to beach the stern on the bank, and held it there with the blades in the mud until Pa was ashore. Lifting the oars free, he climbed out after him.

Once Rust was on land, Pa worked the boat around till he could reach the painter. Pushing her back out, he walked up onto the jetty and bent the painter to a brass ring bolted there. "One ring for fair weather, two for foul," he said, pointing to a second ring further along. "When th' bar goes there's a powerful lot of water pours through here an' she needs tyin' fore an' aft or we risk losin' 'er back t' th' ocean. Wipe th' oars down before you put 'em in."

Rust found some old towelling and was about to start wiping the oars when Pa straightened up and snorted, "What th' devil's that?"

The boy paused and looked about: it was the sound of approaching music. Rust had heard it without being aware of anything odd—the sound of a transistor or tape-player was just an everyday part of his life. "There are two people walking along the banks back there," he said. "It's probably theirs."

"Holiday people!" Pa sniffed. "No right t' foul th' night with that stuff."

Rust finished drying the oars, and put them away just as the two boys who had been using the boat arrived at the head of the jetty. Their portable tape-player with twin speakers was blaring discordant music.

"Turn that damned thing off!" Pa ordered.

The boy carrying it switched it off. "I'm Shaun Taylor, Mr Stewart, and this is Tony Matheson. Dad said we had to come and apologize for taking your boat before. We were just having a bit of a mess-around."

Pa ignored him.

"Dad said if we asked properly you'd let us borrow it."

Tony looked at Rust, and his lip twitched scornfully at the younger boy. Rust looked down quickly. Older Australian boys weren't any different from older American boys, it seemed. He hated being put down.

"Can we?"

Pa shook his head. "Might've, if y'd asked first."

"Oh, thanks a lot," said Shaun. He turned the player up full blast and stepped out onto the jetty.

"Hey! Off m' jetty!"

"Why?" Shaun demanded, the glint of defiance suddenly in his eye. "It's not private property. Come on, Tone."

"It *is* private property!" Pa snapped. "An' turn that damned thing off till you're well away from me." He moved towards the offender.

Rust stepped back against the locker. "Pa," he pleaded, wanting to tell him to just leave the boys alone. But the old man lunged forward and caught Shaun by the arm. "Pa!"

"Ow!" Shaun yelped, in pain.

"Leave 'im alone," Tony shouted, jumping to the fore and catching hold of Pa's arm.

"Why, y' cheeky young monkey!" Pa snarled, and flinging his arm back sent Tony sprawling.

"Shaun!" cried Tony, scrambling to his feet. "He'll kill ya!"

Shaun jumped away from Pa and sprinted back along the bank for twenty or thirty paces, Tony behind him. Then he stopped and turned round. "Crazy old bastard! You wait'll I tell dad!"

"Come on, Pa," Rust urged. "Before he gets his father."

Pa looked at him, then reached out and gripped Rust's shoulder. "Don't you be frightened for me, son." He checked the knot, stepped from the jetty, and started along the bank in the direction of the boys.

"Pa!"

"Shaun!" Tony shouted above the sound of the radio. "He's after us!"

"Stuff off, ya silly old bastard!" Shaun cried out. Then he turned and ran.

"I'll be along t' see y' father t'morrer!" Pa thundered, and stopped, turning after a moment and heading for the entrance to the track. "Come on, son," he said, drawing a deep breath. "Let's get home an' have some of your news from over there."

Chapter Two

Rust rolled over and checked his watch again. Five-forty, though it felt more like mid-afternoon—which it would be in Boston, with snow lining the branches of the maple outside his window, even if it had not snowed again since he'd left home three days ago.

The kids would be out sledding now.

He looked to the window. Sunrise; the tips of the higher leaves tinged with gold beyond the shadow of the house, the breeze already warm through the mosquito netting Pa had fitted, too warm to try to go back to sleep in.

He got up and pulled on shorts and sneakers, not bothering with a top, and crossed to the bathroom, then dashed along to the kitchen. The presents he had brought out last night were still arranged on the table; but there was no sign of either of his great-grandparents, so he went back to his room, took off the window screen and leaned out across the sill.

There was a different smell on the breeze this morning, not salty or musty at all. He smiled, remembering the scent of the eucalyptus trees in California from which both Dad and Grandad collected leaves whenever they went to the west. They said that burning them was like going home. He sniffed the inland breeze: to him it was like being in California!

He grinned and inclined his head to listen again, but there were still no sounds from inside. He really couldn't go back to sleep now, and he didn't just want to hang around...

He slipped over the sill and ran round the back, taking the track to the vegetable garden and squatting down by the strawberries. He selected half-a-dozen pink ones, because he liked them a little tart, and pulled out a carrot before he was away again down the tunnel-path towards the Inlet. The open ground on the bank sprang suddenly with rabbits, their white tails disappearing among the tussocks like scattering golfballs.

An exclamation of surprise escaped from his mouth, and he stopped to see if the rabbits would reappear. They didn't, so he galloped on to the jetty, ran right out to the end, dropped down with his feet dangling over the edge and bit into a strawberry.

The swans were feeding along the edges of the swamps, big black birds with red beaks; majestic birds, dwarfing the tiny grey grebe, which dived in and stayed under for so long that you were convinced they must surely have some secret underwater cave, when up they popped back to the surface.

There would be duck somewhere too, and cormorant, and blue heron, and perhaps egret and ibis — it depended on the amount of water inland, Dad said.

Suddenly, Rust's eye was caught by a white hawklike bird that swept in from the ocean high above the bar, hovering briefly before it dived, breaking the surface of the rippled Inlet without a splash and reappearing seconds later with a silver fish flapping sparklet drops of water in its desperation to break free. A Caspian tern! The sea-swallow he had seen in the lakes and coastal waters back home.

"Hi!" he shouted, and laughed, and climbed up, and went back to look down at the *Clinker*, listening to the gentle *slap-slap-slap* of water against her hull. Then he was off again, tossing the carrot greens to the bank for the rabbits as he ran. He would go and see the old signal station!

He raced past the tangle behind the Robertses' house,

past the two new beach-houses—and for a moment the brightness of the morning dimmed at the memory of what had happened at the jetty last night. Would Pa really go and see Mr Taylor? But his first sight of boiling surf above the bar brought back the brightness and the boy jumped down to the sandy beach and clambered up the steep entrance to the path leading to the station.

"Ssssskit!" he hissed as a rabbit shot from the path ahead into the stunted heathland. He sucked in a huge breath as the steepness of the path drained his energy and had to stop for a few seconds before going on at a walk, becoming aware of the wind now that he was beyond the shelter of the tea-tree. Dad was right, a north wind *was* soft and dry; silky-soft—though he said it lost that silkiness soon after sunrise and became harsh and annoying.

Rust walked from the path onto the patch of bare, rain-washed clay where the old signal station stood. Cut from soft yellow stone, it rose about four metres in a square some three metres across, with a doorway in the side he now faced.

He went in, climbed the steep steps to the top and straddled the wall.

There had probably been a wooden second storey, Dad said, though there was nothing to show it now. But even at this height the structure gave a wide view across the ocean, and Rust wished for a fleet of sealers' boats that he could signal in to safe anchor.

He looked to the southern horizon, the sky so blue and pure in the early-morning light that he found himself smiling. Then he looked down towards the ranges, and was surprised how sharply they stood out this morning. The long curve of the beach that began at their feet was clearly visible now that the mist had lifted.

The ocean itself was almost flat until it neared the beach, where the waves stood tall, green and brittle-thin as they ran in against the northerly, fracturing finally along their crests and smoking away on the wind until the whole long line of them, drawn too thin to roll, tipped over and fell with a crack so sharp it reached him as the sound of a pistol-shot.

He squinted again. There were two surfers out there, trying for the short rides which were all that these waves would give. Maggie and her father? Would he get a chance to surf here before he left? The kids back home would never believe it if he came back raving about this beach and then said he hadn't surfed it—although surfing had hardly entered his mind when he'd been planning the trip; surfing and Pa and Ma and their life didn't seem to belong on the same planet.

He shrugged, and was about to climb down when he saw two other figures standing on the ridge of the dunes. Holiday people? He watched them make their way down to the beach, leaving something on the dry sand before going on into the water; backing away . . . standing. . .

Surf-fishing, of course!

It annoyed him to have all these people about. He'd expected Maggie, but no-one else. The Inlet belonged to Ma and Pa.

Rust looked down towards the house, and saw a waft of blue smoke rise and melt away on the wind. One of them was up and had started the fire. He swung his leg over and backed down the steps and out onto the clay scour again, aware that his skin was tight and stinging. Better go back and get a T-shirt.

Down the narrow path he could run with long, free strides—seven-league boots, almost!—until he was nearly at the steep drop to the beach and had to brake and use his heels as skids. Then off he loped across the sand, hesitating momentarily because he really wanted to go down to the beach, but going on for the house instead because they might be wondering. . .

"Yankee poodle!" a sharp voice jeered.

Rust stumbled in surprise, but recovered without

stopping, from the corner of his eye seeing Shaun on the deck of the house to his right.

"Get off our bank!" Shaun called mockingly. "It's private property!"

Pa hadn't said anything about the riverbank being private property. But he had chased Shaun and Tony off the jetty. Perhaps the house-blocks ran right down to the water.

Rust sprinted past the other new house, slowed right down past Mr Roberts's, Bob's—*he* wouldn't mind, it was Ma's house, anyway—and turned into the track, stopping to look back when the tea-tree reached head-height. Those two kids better not mess up his holiday! Ma had mentioned in her letters that Pa didn't like the arrival of the city people and the talk of a new road and powerlines to service the blocks cut up along the river-bank. She had warned that the new houses had spoilt things a little, but not too much: she said she enjoyed a chance to meet new people now and then . . .

He sighed and went on up the track. Well, it could certainly spoil things for *him*, if it went on like this.

"Rust! We thought you were still asleep." Ma hugged him, releasing him quickly when he winced. "You've been out in the sun! It doesn't take long with a north wind on a day like this. You must wear a shirt."

"Good morning. I didn't think it would get hot so early."

"You've come straight from winter," Pa said. "You'll have t' break y'self in easy." He reached for a slice of bread. "Right, I'll start makin' th' toast."

"I'll just put a shirt on," Rust replied, then remembered. "Pa, do the blocks go right down to the water's edge?"

"Eh? How d'you mean?"

"I was running back from the old signal station and that boy Shaun told me to get off their land."

"By crikey!" Pa rumbled. "Did 'e, eh! No, by George! Their land ends well back from th' banks. I'll make that plain too when I go round there after breakfast. Fact is, I might go down there right now."

"No," Ma stated with authority. "Breakfast; and then we'll call America. Hurry along, son."

Breakfast was porridge and toast, the milk so rich that Rust considered adding water; but that seemed too odd. "It's about as thick as some of the cream we get at home," he said.

"Good pasture, that," Pa explained. "Built it up till I had th' finest pullin' teams in th' Otways. An' now *cows* are thrivin' on it." He sounded sad for a moment, and Rust noticed the quick pat Ma gave him, the little smile of understanding and shared memory. He too felt sad, and was relieved when they had finished eating and could make the phonecall.

That was strange, really weird: standing in a kitchen in Australia and talking to Mom and knowing she was upside down to him, the soles of their feet facing each other through the earth.

"I'm sunburnt already," he told her. "Just from this morning."

"And *I* nearly got frostbite! It's turned into a blizzard. Madelaine and Tim came by; you promised to say goodbye."

"Aw, gee, say I'm sorry when you see them."

"Sure. Is everything the same as you thought it would be?"

"Kind of. The same but, you know, different."

"You're making great sense! Put Ma on. And have a wonderful time."

"Okay, Mom. See ya."

Ma took the phone, and Rust realized that Pa was not there. "He's phone-shy," she explained, gesturing towards the back door as she put the receiver to her ear.

But Rust, a sinking sensation in his chest, did not wait

to hear what Ma might have to say. Pa was probably on his way to see Mr Taylor! He *had* to go with him, whatever he felt.

He ran from the house and down through the tea-tree tunnel, but there was no sign of Pa along the bank. Surely he couldn't have got there this quickly. He was about to press on when it struck him that Pa would have used the road, so he sprinted back and along past the side of the house, reaching the road in time to see Pa turn off, and catching up just as the old man knocked on the door.

"Y' didn't have t' come," Pa said, but in a way which made Rust realize he was glad he had. Or perhaps even proud.

A dark-haired, heavily built man wearing thongs, with a large stomach bulging from a T-shirt over the waistband of an old pair of shorts, answered the door. "G'day, Mr Stewart. I was coming along later to have a word to you. Didn't think you'd be up yet. The boys shouldn't have taken your boat without asking, but that's no reason for you to use physical violence against them."

"I told 'em t' get off my jetty, an' they refused. Least, your son did."

"I sent them down to apologize and said you might lend them your boat—"

"And I said no."

"Well, that's your privilege. But you've got no right to knock my lad down."

"Didn't knock him down, I pushed him away," Pa replied. "I just wanted him off *my* jetty."

Rust could see the two boys grinning in the background, and wanted to reach out and tug Pa away. He was too old to fight. It wasn't worth fighting over, anyway.

"Now listen, Mr Stewart, I know the Inlet's been your private little haven for a long while now, but times are changing. We don't want to throw any weight around, but the fact is that jetty's on public land. You'll just have

to accept that and make the best of it. If someone decides
to go out on your jetty—"

"I'll throw 'em off," Pa cut in, his voice rising. "And if
your son an' his friend play their damn wireless like that
while they're anywhere near me or m' house, I'll throw
that out into th' Inlet too!"

"Now listen here, Mr Stewart." Shaun's father took a
step forward. "You might be an old man—"

He should never have said that, Rust knew, even before
Pa moved.

"Dad!" Shaun cried out as his father stumbled back
into the house. "You can't hit my father!"

"I didn't hit him, son," Pa answered, his voice low
now, low and reasonable and under control. "I pushed
him, flat hand. If I'd hit him. . ." He shook his head. "An'
don't you come down anywhere near m' jetty or m' boat
or m' land, or you'll get what I promised."

"I oughta. . ." Mr Taylor rasped, his voice shaking. "I
oughta. . ." But he didn't make any move to come
forward, and Pa turned, put a hand on Rust's shoulder
and moved him away.

"Come on, son. There's a lot t' do while you're here."
He didn't even look back. "I reckon you an' I ought t' go
fishin'." They walked off side by side.

"Pa, why don't you come over and live in America,"
Rust managed in a shaky voice he was ashamed of,
"where you've got a whole family?"

"Reckon I can still take care of y' Ma an' me all right,
son. Maybe when I'm on me last legs, it might be an idea
to come over so she'll have someone when I'm gone. But
I think that's a bit further along th' track yet." He was
silent for several paces. "Though I don't know how much
more I can stand th' sight of that young fella an' others
like 'im walkin' *bored* round this Inlet with a music-box.
Y' grandfather *and* y' father never had enough hours in
th' day t' do all they wanted t' when they was here."

Rust snatched a glance back along the road as they turned in at the gate.

"An' don't go 'earin' footsteps an' lookin' back—that means they've beat y'," said Pa. "Nellie, reckon I'll take th' boy out an' show 'im what th' fishin's like."

"I was going to take him down to the Robertses' with Maggie's present," Ma said, coming to the back door.

"All right, you do that while I dig up some worms. Then I'll have a cuppa with you before we go."

"Has someone been upsetting you?" she asked, suddenly concerned.

He reached out and touched the side of her face gently with his fingers. "Don't you go worryin' about me, Nell."

"I try not to. Go on, Rust. You go and get the worms with him. I'll change and get a cup of tea ready for Pa while we're gone. You needn't stay down there. I just want to show you off!"

Rust smiled quickly, and turned and followed his great-grandfather down to the shed. Its timbers had the same look as the furniture in his bedroom, only paler and unrubbed.

"Did this timber come from the *Ohio* too, Pa?"

"Most things come from th' *Ohio* except for th' house itself." He leaned a shoulder against the door jamb. "Most things," he repeated, "an' sometimes, of a wild storm night, I reckon th' sailors come too. Sound of Yankee voices in th' wind, at times." He frowned, and his eyes seemed to look away into a distance beyond the trees. "Sometimes I wonder if those same voices are what took my boy away t' America. A man never knows in this life. Stranger tales than that 'ave been told of shipwreck."

Rust felt a cold shiver through the warmth of his body. "Really, Pa? Do you really think that?"

His great-grandfather dropped his head and looked at him, appearing to have trouble focusing; then he coughed and cleared his throat and pushed open the door. "Not today. Not on a bright clear day. Then I tell m'self it's just plain foolishness." He reached for a shovel and can, brought them out, paused again, and again seemed to lose himself in some other . . . place? "But come a wild storm night . . . well, then I get t' wonderin' again an' half believin' if that was th' sailors' way of gettin' themselves back home."

"And . . . now that Dad and Grandad are over there, do you still hear the voices?"

Pa sighed. "That's th' strange thing. I *think* I hear 'em, then I find it's not really them at all an' I begin t' wonder if it ever was. . ."

He turned abruptly, led the way down to the vegetable garden, and pointed to a partly rotten bag spread on the ground. "Ease that bag aside an' put a shovel in there."

Rust dug, and his shovel turned up a mass of red earthworms.

"Get about half a tinful an' cover 'em with some of that rot there. Heat will shrivel 'em. Put th' bag back quick as you can too."

"Did you ever get spooked by those voices, Pa?" Rust asked as they walked back to the shed.

Pa shrugged, and put the shovel away. "I guess sometimes it was enough t' have me stay up most of th' night with a fire goin'. Used t' think about how it would be t' run up on a reef in heavy seas an' be thrown into th' boil of a storm when y' ship broke up under y'. Used t' worry me a lot on th' nights when I thought th' voices were callin'." He pointed into the shed. "Put th' worms in there till you get back from y' visitin'."

Rust ran through the kitchen. "I'll just change my socks, Ma." But that wasn't the real reason why he wanted to go to his room for a moment: Pa's words were disturbing.

He ran a hand over the smooth wood of the chest of drawers. It was hard to imagine that this was once part of a ship being beaten to pieces on the Tambourine.

Had there really been spirits on the storm winds? *No!*

There were no such things as spirits. Not spirits of dead sailors on the wind, anyway. He ran back, to a glass of milk and a hunk of new bread smeared thickly with butter and apricot jam.

"Pa said to feed you up so you wouldn't stay for morning tea at the Robertses'."

"Might go down an' get a few things ready an' wait for you there," Pa said. "See if Maggie'll come with you an' we'll get a feed of bream for both houses."

Ma filled a bowl of strawberries from the fridge. "I always like to take something," she explained. "Now go and fetch the present you brought for Maggie."

It was strange walking along a sandy track with Ma in a fresh black dress and a hat. It was as if they were going to church, and Rust felt suddenly conscious of his shorts and T-shirt.

"Should I run back and change?"

She smiled. "You're dressed just right. It's because I never seem to go anywhere except these visits anymore that I like to dress up a little."

He nodded, relieved. "Ma, did you ever hear the voices of the dead sailors in the wind on storm nights?"

"The voices of the men from the *Ohio*?" She frowned. "Who knows? Don't you go filling your head with such things."

"But . . . you might have?"

"Mm, perhaps. It would seem a little strange, with so many drowned along these shores in the past, if some of them didn't find themselves lost and come seeking a little human comfort."

"Pa says he thinks the voices stopped when Grandad took his family to America."

"Mm, that's what he thinks, and perhaps he's right."

"But you've heard them, or others, since?"

"I don't know, Rust. When you get to my age you sometimes hear things that aren't sounds, and see things that aren't there."

"But you must have heard them before Dad went to America, and you weren't old then."

Ma shook her head and quickened her pace. "There are things we simply know nothing of, and I'm content to leave it that way. We can't expect to know everything."

Rust realized that Ma didn't want to keep talking about it. But if there was going to be a storm while he was here, he would listen very closely.

They turned in through the picket fence, its gate, like the other, also hanging awry with a rusted hinge, and went along a path around the side of the house to a corrugated-iron lean-to protecting the back door.

"Hello, Mrs Stewart. Come in."

"I've brought our Russell over to meet you, Anne."

"Hello, Russell. They've really been looking forward to your coming. Let's go into the kitchen."

The room was similar in shape to the one they had just left. Pa had built both the houses at the same time, this one as a present for Ma to give her an income of her own. But only the shape was the same. Mrs Roberts had decorated it with macrame hangings, strange pottery and paintings (which Rust guessed she had done herself), and wall-hangings of driftwood and beads. A spinning-wheel was set up in one corner with a basket of wool ready to be spun, and there was a loom with a guitar resting on it. The floor was covered with handmade rugs.

Hippiesville, he thought; just like some of the tourist traps he had been in at home.

"Maggie brought the milk, but she wouldn't stop and talk," Ma said, putting the bowl of strawberries on the table beside a wooden butter-churn.

Anne Roberts's laugh was deep and low. "She's jealous of Rust. She thinks she owns you, Mrs Stewart. Have a seat."

Rust held out the present. "Mom and Dad sent this for her."

Mrs Roberts smiled, a smile as deep as her laugh, and

Rust dropped his eyes, embarrassed but not sure why; and confused, because somehow he had never thought of finding someone like this in Australia—certainly not someone Ma and Pa knew. The long straight hair falling down to meet the equally long full dress with the bare feet showing just occasionally below the hem seemed again to belong to someone on a hippie commune. And he'd thought that was native America.

"Pa said to see if Maggie would come fishing with us."

"She's somewhere out the back. Why don't you go and find her?"

"Then go on back to Pa," Ma said, realizing he was uncomfortable here. "Anne and Bob might come over one evening and have a sing-song with us on the guitar. We'll have a meal and you can get to know them properly."

"Uh, great. I'll see you then, Mrs Roberts." Rust backed gratefully to the door. "Thanks," he added. He wasn't sure what for, it just seemed to slip out. "See ya."

He pushed the outside door closed and fled down a track that seemed to lead towards the Inlet, not worrying about Maggie. He didn't particularly want her to come anyway. But a minute later he jerked to a stop as two bare legs and then a body dropped from a tree ahead, and Maggie was standing there in front of him, head on one side, hands on hips, challenging him in some way.

"Uh, Pa wants you to come fishing with us."

"He's not my pa," she said, and slipped away through the brush.

"Mom and Dad said to say thankyou for visiting them. Maggie?"

She didn't stop and she didn't answer. Rust clenched his fists in frustration and continued on down the track, angry suddenly because now *she* was spoiling it too.

"C'mon, son," Pa called, sighting him from the jetty. "Fish'll be dead of old age afore we get t' 'em!"

Rust broke into a run through the tussocks. Pa was

already in the stern, and Rust shoved the bow off the mud and climbed aboard onto his knees. "Maggie wouldn't come."

"Devil of a girl t' understand," Pa muttered.

"Where are we going?" Rust asked quickly, unshipping the oars. He didn't want to discuss Maggie.

"Upstream. I'll show you th' creek an' th' land. But take it easy. It's a long pull."

They went up past the swamps and into the creek that fed the Inlet, under the wooden bridge that carried the highway, and along the winding stream. The edges of the water on either side were thick with coarse reeds and a short bamboo-like grass, which hosted small birds in tiny hanging nests above the water and provided escape for the little grebe that slipped in between the stalks on the corrugations of the *Clinker*'s passing. The land beyond the edges of the banks, on the wide, flat valley floor, was tangled grasslands with young trees beginning to grow in patches.

All at once Pa put a finger to his lips and indicated for Rust to stop rowing and stand and look. Three grey forester kangaroos stood motionless a hundred metres or so across from the creek, their heads turned towards the boat, their ears pointing.

"Wow!"

At the sound of Rust's voice their heads turned away and they moved off, slow, almost undulating, without panic.

"It's different from seeing them in parks," Rust said, watching. "Dad never said anything about kangaroos being on your paddocks."

Pa laughed softly. "Because they weren't. Grass was a bit too valuable for feedin' th' roos as well as th' teams so I used t' keep 'em shot off. They still hadn't got used t' th' idea they was welcome, even when your father'd left. Used t' be a picture, these paddocks—even better than Charley Link up at th' dairy keeps th' hillside now he's got it f'r his cows. Wants t' buy th' flats too, but I tell him I've got a great-grandson who just might want them one day."

Rust sat and lifted the oars again, wishing Pa wouldn't say things like that. It only made them both regretful. "I'm sure to end up working in space technology, Pa," he said quietly. "I want to try and get into the Naval Academy at Annapolis. Dad says I might even get to go to Mars, if I do."

"That's a long way for a woodcutter's great-grandson."

Rust's enthusiasm overtook the sadness, and he nodded. "Maybe I can be one of the explorers on Mars who get to name a place. If I do I'm going to call it after you."

"Me?"

"Dad says you're the spirit of the Stewarts. He says it's you and Ma who've made us all want to succeed. Do you wish you'd had the chance to go to Mars, Pa?"

The old man smiled and slowly shook his head. "I was pretty full up cuttin' a livin' out of new land, son. But I wasn't content t' stay in th' city where I grew up, so maybe goin' t' Mars is not all that different t' what I did in my day. Maybe the Stewarts *have* got pioneerin' blood in their veins, eh?"

"Yeah." Rust glanced behind to check his way. The creek had become very narrow now: he could almost touch the banks with the blades. "How much further can we go?"

"Not much. Turn 'er in t' th' bank on th' next turn an' we'll see who's hungry."

Rust pulled the bow into the reeds above the next bend and shipped the oars. Pa was already threading a worm, and Rust picked up the rod Pa had set up for him and baited it. "Do we cast?"

"Just drop 'er in. Too many snags if y' hook somethin' much away from th' boat. Bait up th' other line too, an' just rest 'em. Probably be bream, an' they don't like th' feel of a hand on th' line. They take th' bait in their lips an' swim with it for a bit t' check before they bite on it, so you've got t' leave 'em a bit of slack t' play with."

Rust rested his rod against the gunwale, pulled some line from the reel and let it lie in the bottom of the boat. He baited up the other rod.

"Did you used to work down this end of the valley at all, Pa?"

"Mm. Some good trees along th' creek here when I come. Red ironbarks, like th' ones y' can see runnin' right across th' hill there. Same kind, I mean, not size. These are th' young'uns of th' ones I brought down. They built a lot of bridges an' laid a lot of railroad track on th' timber I took out of th' bush here."

"It must have been hard work."

"Muscle work, an' good work, knowin' you were helpin' build up a new country. Be th' same feelin' you'll have up there in th' sky when you're cuttin' out a new place for us t' spread. Grab y' rod, he's got th' lot!"

Rust snatched his mind back from a vision of the Red Planet, made a move towards one rod, realized it was the wrong one, fumbled the other, and managed to get a hold as the reel began to spin against the ratchet.

"Don't jerk 'im! Slow 'im down, then tire 'im."

Rust braked the reel gently with the palm of his hand against the drum, slipped his fingers around to the handle and wound a turn as the rod bent—and the vibration of the fish running at the other end sent a thrill through his arms into his body.

"Looks like a nice one. Got a good bow in y' rod. Take 'im easy, but don't let 'im get too far away."

The fish made a sudden run to one side, the taut line sizzling through the water, and Rust followed it with the tip of the bowed rod, releasing a little more line but making the fish work for it, reeling in a few turns when the pressure eased.

"One more run an' I reckon he'll be ready t' come in,"

Pa said. He reached for the landing-net. "Make 'im really work on this one, son."

Rust took in several metres of line as the fish came back towards them, maintaining the tension till the fish changed direction and ran out, then sideways, and the line sprayed water where it sliced the surface.

But this run didn't last—Rust could *feel* the spirit going out of the fish—and when it stopped, and he began to wind, the rod was hardly bowed.

"Good one! Go a pound an' a half, I reckon." Pa was pleased as he slipped the net under the silver body and lifted it into the boat. "Give 'im a hit with th' mallet so he doesn't suffer, an' we'll see if any of his mates are around. They feed in shoals."

They took another four, not quite so big, before turning back for home. The north wind had eased but the air felt no cooler and they were both thirsty, in spite of drinking from the creek.

"You'll need a good feed after all this rowin'," Pa remarked as they re-entered the Inlet and rounded the swamps. "Like t' give th' sail a try after lunch?"

"Yeah!" Rust was full of enthusiasm; but they took an hour off after they had eaten just sitting in the cool of the kitchen while the boy answered questions about the others at home.

"I better have a go at that top hinge, too," Pa reminded himself when they were ready to go back to the water. "Got a feelin' they'll want t' know that's on before you leave."

Down by the jetty Ma found herself a place in the shade of the tree by the locker, and Pa helped Rust to get out the gear. "Bring her into th' bank."

Rust undid the painter and walked the *Clinker* along to the bank. He hauled her broadside up onto the mud, and together they lifted the mast into the hole in her bow decking and fitted the boom.

"There's only th' one mast lashing," Pa said as they

hoisted the sail. "Spills a lot of wind, but I built her so she'd be quick an' easy for a boy t' rig by himself. Swing her out an' I'll pass you th' rest of th' gear from th' jetty."

Once Rust was aboard, Pa shoved her off, walked her out to the jetty with the painter and tied her there. Rust left the sail riding out on the boom while he took the rudder and tiller and pinned them in, then slid the two leeboards into their brass fittings beside the rowlock blocks.

"Only use your leeward board. You've got t' change them about when you cross th' wind."

"I know. Dad said he forgot once and broke a bracket."

"An' was too frightened t' tell your Pa for a week," Ma called.

Pa handed down the painter. Rust took it, made his way back to the stern, threaded the mainsheet through its pulley and tightened the sail. With the wind offshore he was able to let the Clinker run without any boards down at all, and he waited till he was well out before he leaned forward and pushed the board in on the lee side and felt it bite as the boat, hard against the water at both centre and stern, shook her head and began to run.

Rust smiled, and tightened the sail until white spray cut away from her bow. He put the tiller over and brought her round, fumbling for several moments as he worked out the moves to change the leeboards before getting her set and cutting back towards the jetty.

He drove close in, so that he could grin—he couldn't afford a hand to wave—to show his great-grandparents how much he was enjoying it. Then he set a course that would take him up past the swamps to the very head of the Inlet, with the wind directly to starboard; a wind that came in across the heads of the forest giants and swept their perfume to the ocean beyond the dunes. He must go out and really explore the ocean beaches soon...

Suddenly there was a sharp, sickening thud and Rust

gripped the gunwale in alarm. A large stone crashed and skidded off the *Clinker*'s bow and splashed into the water. The scented air was pierced by a harsh voice.

"We're gonna *get* you and the old man!"

Chapter Three

Was it just a threat to frighten him or would they really try something to get back at Pa and himself?

The question disturbed Rust's sleep, and he woke early again the next morning when he would rather not have. The Boston clock in his head was still resisting the change to Australian time.

Ma had suggested he stay in bed this morning until she got up, to try to force his body to make the adjustment. But there was no chance of going back to sleep, so he lay there watching the unmoving leaves of the tea-tree against the first browning of the morning sky, wondering what the Taylor boy and his friend might try to do, wishing he could just forget them.

He sighed and forced his mind back to the new day around him. The north wind must have blown itself out in the night. He turned his head slightly, aware of the distant surf: a sharp cracking this morning, as if the waves were smaller. Or was it something to do with the lack of breeze?

He grinned and drew in a long breath of contentment, then turned his head quickly at a sound from the door.

"Awake?" Pa whispered. "Get on some clothes an' we'll go an' get us a rabbit."

Rust rolled from the bed. "Ouch!" The sunburn bit his shoulders.

"Burnt?"

"It's not bad once I've moved it."

"Be in th' kitchen."

"'K." Rust changed out of his pyjamas, watching his

reflection in the brass of the *Ohio*'s lamp. He slipped across to the bathroom to cool his face with a wet flannel, before making his way to the kitchen. "Ready."

Pa slid three shells from a box into his pocket. "Ever used a twelve-gauge? Twelve-*bore*, I think you call 'em over there." He lifted the gun from the table and sighted down the insides of the barrels.

"I've only used an air-rifle."

"Have t' try your size on a real gun, then. Just remember t' keep th' butt well into your shoulder." He stood and crooked the gun over one arm and led the way out. "You've got t' aim a bit high. Not like a rifle trajectory. We'll go down th' track t' th' bank."

"I saw them there yesterday."

"Yeh. Good spot for a pot at a bunny." Pa walked carefully, so as not to snap a twig or rustle a branch, and stopped just past the shed. "I'll put two shells in." He slipped them into the breeches and snapped the hammers back. "Carry it broken till you're right at th' end of th' track, then close it an' shoot, because they'll hear th' click an' won't wait around scratchin' themselves."

Rust nodded and took the gun, surprised by its weight.

"Soon as you've had your shot, one or both, break 'er again before you move. That's for safety."

The boy went quietly down the track, breathing the cool, sweet air, noticing the taste of salt in it and realizing that the north wind was well gone, the sharp crack of the breakers crisper out here than from his bedroom. A vision of the Tambourine Reef crossed his mind, but he pushed it away and concentrated on the track, crouching for concealment as the level of the tea-tree canopy fell, then dropping to one knee as the bank came into full view.

There were at least a dozen rabbits feeding amongst the tussocks, their high, rounded hindquarters and bright tails moving in small half-hops as they changed feeding-patches, their ears close-held except when they flicked at an annoying insect.

He eased the gun closed, and the metallic click was like an electric shock through the game: most of the rabbits froze instantly. But one, a big buck, came upright, ears high, and thumped the ground in warning with one back leg as Rust sighted him between the barrels and squeezed.

The mighty *ka-boom* of the explosion shattered the calm. Simultaneously, the butt of the gun drove back into Rust's shoulder, throwing him off-balance. His finger gripped spasmodically, bringing back the other trigger, and the second explosion rolled out to meet the echoes of its twin as Rust went over on his back. "Ow!" he cried, letting the gun fall across his stomach and grabbing at his shoulder.

"Son. . .?" Pa shouted in concern, easing into a heavy run down the track. "Son, what's up?"

"I'm all right," Rust called, sitting, seeing the startled swans rising above the dunes as they fled in fright. "I pulled the second trigger by accident. Ouch! I wasn't holding it into my shoulder."

Pa bent and took the gun. "Should'a thought t' warn you about th' two triggers."

"It was more the shock," Rust winced, massaging. "I was off-balance. Did I get one?"

Pa looked across the bank. "Yep. There 'e is, tonight's tea. Good big fella. I'll go an' get 'im."

"I will." Rust got up. "Ouch! It's set the sunburn off." He ran out across the bank and picked up the rabbit by its hind legs. All at once he regretted shooting it.

"Got t' keep 'em down," Pa said loudly, sensing the boy's feelings. "They brought 'em over from England a hundred an' fifty years ago an' they bred up t' a plague an' nearly ruined th' country. Would have, if th' scientists hadn't come up with a disease that near finished 'em." He waved a wide sweep with one arm. "They had all this down t' bare sand an' blowin' away. Better be sure you don't take anything like that up t' Mars when you go."

"No." Rust felt better about the animal that now hung limp from his hand, and ran back.

"Brought out for hunting. A bit of sport. Them an' foxes an' they *both* ran plague-wild. How's th' shoulder now?"

"Just a bit bruised. It's not worrying me."

They walked back to the shed, where Pa leaned the gun and took out a pocketknife. He pulled out the smaller of the two blades. "Show you how t' skin a bunny." He marked the skin around the back legs and slit in to the crotch, stripped back the skin from the two legs, cut the base of the tail, and peeled the skin from the steaming pink body. Another nick on the inside near the ears and the entire skin slipped over the head. "Like t' set a craypot? Get me a tin."

Rust brought one from inside the shed. Pa slit the rabbit up the centre and tipped the gut in, then sliced off the head and feet and added them. "Find a bit of bagging t' keep th' flies off. We'll get Ma t' go down an' show you where t' set th' pot right after breakfast."

"Was that you shooting?" Ma asked as they came in. "I thought I heard *both* barrels," she added, seeing the rabbit.

"I slipped on the trigger," Rust confessed, embarrassed.

"Should'a just put a single in for his first go," Pa said. "Thought we'd use th' gut t' bait a pot after breakfast, if you feel up t' a bit of rock climbin'."

"How's the tide?" Ma asked.

"About right, I'd say."

Breakfast over, Ma put on her waterboots and they went down to the shed, where Pa took a beautifully bent and woven crayfish pot from a shelf. Rust didn't need to wonder who had made it or where the cane had come from.

"She was a good general store, the *Ohio*," Pa remarked. "Time was, anything you needed you just went down an' dug around till you found it. You bring th' bait."

They carried the pot and the can down to the jetty, and Rust got the oars while Pa walked the *Clinker* in to the bank. "Want me t' row till that shoulder settles down?"

"Nuh. It's all right now."

Pa helped Ma into the boat and climbed after her. Rust pushed off and clambered across to the rowing-seat, and unshipped the oars. "Where do we put the pot, Ma?"

"One of the holes in the tide rocks—I know them all from a lot of years harvesting them with little boys! And keep your sneakers on. The mussel-shells are sharp."

Rust brought the boat broadside to the sand of the bar, climbed out and held it until they were ashore. "You coming too, Alfred?" Ma asked, surprised when he picked up the pot.

"One last time. I been there with a son an' a grandson; reckon I'd like t' make it with a great-grandson too. Once, anyway."

Rust looked away sadly. Pa was old, he knew that; but to hear it spoken of in this way . . .

"Come on, young'un," Pa said, using his stick to help him forward across the deep dry sand.

The boy lifted out the tin of bait and followed across the bar and down to the hard of the ebb on the other side. The walking was easier up along the edge of the mullet run, so shallow now that the water would not come to their ankles if they walked through it to the rocks. Ma turned across and stepped up onto the shelf.

"Give us a hand up son," Pa said, dropping the pot on the rocks.

Rust heaved, and the old man came up and lifted the pot again. They followed Ma out towards the ocean edge, where the water in the fissures welled and sucked at the ebb and flow of the swells.

"What are you looking for, Ma?" Rust asked when she

crouched down and peered into a hole in the rocks, a hole about the size of a bathtub.

"Tracks. Look carefully and you'll see where the crays have been walking."

Rust crouched and looked down through the crystal-clear water, which, he realized with surprise, rose and fell in time with the swells, obviously coming through some tunnel from the outer edge of the shelf. Two, maybe three metres down, the sandy bottom was marked with tracks, but he could not even begin to guess which of them had been made by crayfish.

"I can't either," Pa said, seeming to read his mind, "an' neither could your grandfather. But your father could."

"He had a better eye than I did," Ma put in. "Anyway, they're down there, even if you can't tell, and big ones too."

"You get a rock t' weigh 'er down an' I'll find a hitch, son," Pa told him; but Ma shook her head.

"There," she said, pointing. "That's where we always tied when we potted this hole. And there should be a nice big stone in that shallow hole there, too."

Rust looked, and grinned, bending and lifting the rock out, an odd feeling in his hands as he realized that both his father and his grandfather had probably lifted this same rock from the same hole all those years ago.

He handed it to Pa, who eased it into the pot, and looked on while Ma wired the head and gut of the rabbit onto the base.

"Watch the little fellas," she said, lowering the pot down to the water and letting it go. As it began to sink, the little red bonehead catfish darted from their hideouts below the ledges, slipping between the cane stakes and nipping at the bait.

"We'll leave it there right through the flood," Ma said. "We should have brought a rod and let you try your luck."

"There's th' old devil!" Pa exclaimed suddenly. "See? Where th' water's got a boil on."

Rust stood quickly, not quite sure what to expect, and looked out to sea to where Pa was pointing with his stick, out across the pale blue-and-green of the gentle swells to where the sharp brightness of broken water flashed in the sunlight. "Is that the Tambourine? It doesn't look very dangerous. I mean, it's easy to see."

"When th' water's down," Pa said. "But you'd be a sharp-witted lookout t' spot it on th' flood when she's three, four feet under."

"Have you ever been out there, Pa?"

"Yep, couple of times. Your father an' his father an' I have eased th' *Clinker* out through th' mouth when she's been open, an' rowed there."

"I wish I could go."

"Not a lot t' see. First time I was expectin' bits an' pieces of wreck. But anything left out there must be on th' bottom, or so 'crusted you can't tell."

"Did they bury the sailors here?"

"Well, they say some of those who got ashore put th' others in a shallow grave on th' beach while they went for help," Pa answered. "But there's nothing about comin' back for 'em. Got t' remember this was a long way from civilization in those days—sealers long gone and th' likes of Ma an' me still a long way off comin'. Might've been weeks walkin' in to find anybody. My guess is they never did get back."

"Don't let it prey on your mind, son," Ma said gently. "Let's go back to the beach and see if we can find some shells under the cliffs. I promised your mother I'd send a collection back to her."

They walked back past the bar to the beach at the feet of the cliffs below the old signal station.

"We'll do the tideline while you hunt the pools," Ma said. "Don't take the living shells."

"Think I might just find myself a convenient rock." Pa turned up the beach to an ancient fall of great boulders in the shadow of the cliffs and found himself a seat. "It's a poor job that won't support one boss," he puffed, settling himself.

Rust was not quite sure what Pa meant, but Ma laughed so he did too, and went on with her along the rocky shore, probing the sand of the pools with a piece of driftwood and collecting the vacated homes of shellfish until his pockets were dripping-wet and bulging.

"We'll go back and sort them on the rocks with Pa," Ma called as he reached the end of the point. She had collected hers in a large handkerchief. "I should have thought to bring a basket. It's been so long since I've been down here I'd forgotten all the little preparations I used to make before I set off with one of the boys. I should have brought a picnic lunch too."

"Dad and Grandad both talk about the picnics on the beach. They say it keeps the edges of your teeth sharpened eating sand with everything."

Ma smiled, and they walked slowly back to where Pa sat. "I brought you a nice cuttlebone to whittle," she said, passing it to him before spreading her haul on the top of a flat rock. "I found three cowries." She set the sweetly shaped shells together and began sorting the others. "Lots of periwinkles, these cream ones that look like shells should. And green turbans—they're the ones that have the little white buttons for doors. We used to collect the buttons to use as counters and markers in games."

"What are these called? The patterns look like Persian carpets."

"Pheasants. You get those brown ones quite easily, but the ones with more red in them are hard to find." Ma ran a finger round the smooth, bulging spirals, the patterns even and intricate in three shades of brown, then picked up a small pointed one something like the glass of a

Christmas-tree light. "These are wentletraps; and that's a triton."

"How do you know them all?"

"I've always loved the shore. As soon as your grandfather was old enough to toddle, I made this his playground. It seemed natural to buy some books so I could teach him all there was to know about it."

"She does beautiful pencil drawings of th' shells an' driftwood," Pa said proudly.

Rust beamed. "I know! We've got two framed in our sitting-room at home, and Grandad's got about *twenty* in his study."

Ma flushed slightly, pleased. "Think he could afford better than that by now."

"Aren't any better," Pa said. "Should've brought a picnic," he added, looking around.

"Why don't I row back and get one?" Rust suggested. "Yeah. I wouldn't be long."

"What would you get?" Ma asked.

"Well. . . Bread and butter. Strawberries. A bottle of stone ginger. Cheese. . ."

Ma laughed in delight. "And a fresh lettuce? All right. I'll collect some more shells and Pa can whittle while you're gone."

"I'll be as quick as I can." He galloped back along the dry sand, full of the pleasure of it all. Along under the base of the cliff and up over the bar he sprinted, leaping into the bow of the *Clinker* so that she ran off the sand and went rocking out onto the Inlet while he was still on his knees on the decking.

He scrambled back and unshipped the oars, and was about to pull her head around when the sound of discordant music reached him from somewhere in the dunes to his right. He paused, feeling the elation drain away. Should he leave Ma and Pa alone? He hesitated, then shrugged. What could he do against them anyway? He gritted his teeth in anger and frustration and pulled the boat around, watching the dunes, which were now beside him as he rowed. The dream had come true, he was here, but it wasn't quite the way he had thought it would be. He hadn't figured on any new people, hadn't even thought of them, though Ma had mentioned the changes in her letters.

He glanced left at the sound of a voice. Mr Taylor and a woman—Mrs Taylor, he supposed—were lolling on chairs under a bright beach umbrella set up on their deck. He could have been in a Miami resort! The woman was even waving. He dropped the left oar for long enough to return her wave, feeling obliged to. Why did they want to be down here? There must be plenty of resorts already set up in Australia. Why come and spoil the Inlet?

Rust pulled the *Clinker* in towards the bank beside the jetty. Two fishermen, bristling with short river-rods, were walking along the opposite bank beside the dunes. It was almost *crowded* here! To slip back into the sanctuary of the path was a relief.

He went straight to the vegetable garden and chose a small lettuce; then, holding the bottom of his T-shirt with one hand to make a pouch for the strawberries, he carried them back to the house, not noticing that the back door was already open, but seeing the milk billy on the table and realizing that Maggie had been.

He stood on tiptoe and spilt the strawberries and lettuce onto the draining-board, putting one of the berries into his mouth as he crossed back and picked up the billy to take to the fridge.

"Who's that?" The words jerked out of him, and pink strawberry juice trickled down his lower lip to his chin. "Who is it?" With his free hand he wiped the juice from his mouth and chin, watching the inner door. But there was no answer, and no further sound.

It had probably been something in the ceiling. . .

He continued to the fridge, putting the milk away and

collecting things for the picnic. The billy drew his thoughts to Maggie. He wouldn't tell anyone, but he was rather glad she was jealous—or whatever it was that kept her away. He didn't really want to share Ma and Pa with her, or with anyone. That must be how she felt about *him*, he guessed. Well, she could have them all to herself again once he was gone.

He washed the lettuce and strawberries and found a basket. Ma didn't have any plastic wrap that he could find so he put them into brown-paper bags, aware for the first time of just how little Ma did have in the kitchen. No waste-disposal, no blender or mixer. Not even a hot-water tap over the sink.

Into the basket he put a bottle of stone ginger and three glasses; cheese, bread, knives (the bread knife and the small vegetable knife); and why not three tomatoes? He went back to the fridge and got them, and made up two little paper screws containing salt and pepper.

Now *that* should make a picnic!

He finished packing the basket and was just about to lift it when another sound came from somewhere in the house.

"*Who's that?*" he jerked, and froze for an instant. "I . . . I'm bringing the gun!"

There was a loud crash in response, and Rust bolted. He tried to tell himself he must have left the window of his bedroom open and a bird had come in and knocked something down. But it didn't ring true. Instead, he sensed Pa's ghostly sailors somehow leaking into his mind . . .

Stupid!

But just telling himself he was stupid didn't change anything. He stumbled and ran out across the bank, tripping to his knees as he reached the boat, the glasses ringing together as he almost *threw* the basket in to have his hands free to grasp the gunwale so as to stop himself falling full-length in the water.

Stupid!

He shoved off, riding the bow out on his knees, then scrambling round to the seat and unshipping the oars and hauling with all his strength to get her moving, his eyes fixed on the entrance to the tea-tree track, expecting... What? What could possibly emerge from a track in the middle of the day except another human being? A *live* one.

He made himself look to the Taylors' deck, glad this time to have them there, and steadied his rate. He didn't want them, or anyone, to know of the panic he'd been in.

"You were quick, son."

"I was extra hungry," he lied.

"My, you *have* done us proud," Ma exclaimed, looking into the basket. "Come on, Pa! Down onto the sand for this."

"What do you think of 'er?" Pa asked, passing a tiny white cuttlebone rowboat to Rust.

"Gee! It's . . . beautiful, Pa." He smiled as he turned the carved model round in his hands. "Exactly the *Clinker*."

"I'll fix 'er up with a couple of bits of brass wire an' some wood oars when we get home. Take 'er back for a memory."

"Thanks!"

"Oof! Haven't been down on th' sand in a long time," Pa gruffed as he eased himself from the rock. "Think I must be gettin' old, Nellie."

"You're only a boy," she laughed, and Rust looked quickly away when he saw the sudden glisten of tears in her eyes. Pa *was* old; at eighty-five and eighty-two, they both were.

"And tomatoes!" Ma said enthusiastically. "Give Pa the ginger to open, and then find me some nice big flat rocks for plates."

Rust passed the bottle to his great-grandfather and scrambled down the sand on all fours towards the sea.

"Under the cliffs, son," Ma called.

He spun round on his hands and took off back up the beach to the base of the cliffs, surprised to see the paving of flat oval dark-grey stones up to the size of dinner-plates.

"Coast crockery—won't rust!" Pa called. "Fresh washed twice a day." Rust grinned, stacked four suitable ones and staggered back with them.

"An' that driftwood plank over there for a cuttin' board," Pa added, waving his stick. "Pre-salts th' sandwiches."

They had hardly begun slicing the bread when the *cark-cark* of a silver gull came from above them, and within minutes a dozen of the birds stood about on the sand or hovered above their heads.

"Won't get much from us, lads," Pa called. "Man's too hungry t' feed scavengers—'less y' th' ghosts of th' drowned."

"Pa," Ma reprimanded him. "None of that on a picnic."

He grunted, and threw a twist of crust; and the other two joined him, trying to see how close they could make the birds come, though Rust found that he suddenly did not want them too close at all, that he felt uneasy...

"I like the little hooded dotterels and the sandpipers best," Ma said. "Trouble is, I'm a little too stiff these days to go along the open beaches looking for them, but you might like to. You might even find a nest, if you keep your eyes skinned. Take your lunch one day and walk right up to the end of the long beach. Your grandfather and your father and I often spent a whole day on that walk, just exploring the dunes and the flood tideline for treasures—like those sea-dragons hanging in your room."

"It's just th' life for a growin' boy," Pa said enthusiastically. "Though it took me time t' break your grandfather into work when we decided he was old enough t' help earn his keep."

"No it didn't," Ma disagreed. "Once he was allowed to work with the horses I never could get him back on the beach. If the war hadn't come I think he'd still be out there in the bush."

Pa frowned, looking uncomfortable. "Weren't th' war. I reckon it was th' sailors." He cleared his throat, then coughed, lifting his head with deep frowning eyes towards the horizon. "Reckon there's a sea fog comin' in."

"Well, I don't want you . . . we don't any of us want to be out here when it comes." Ma was visibly worried.

Rust stood up, a chunk of bread in one hand, a half-eaten tomato in the other, and looked. A great bank of brown-grey was hanging above the ocean. "Will it come right in here?"

"Might," Ma said, already beginning to pack. "On clear days like this it can come in so dense you can feel it sticky on your skin and can't see halfway across the Inlet."

Rust took a bite of bread and a bite of tomato and chewed them together, then bent and added a strawberry while he watched the bank. It was not a static blanket, as he had first thought, but a great heavy mass that appeared to be rolling in towards them.

Pa coughed again, and Ma clattered the glasses in her haste. "Help me, Rust."

He dropped to his knees, surprised by the tenseness in her voice, and helped her to gather and pack while Pa heaved himself unsteadily to his feet. "Feel it on me chest already."

"You start off right away," Ma told him. "Go on, Alfred. Quick!"

"No need t' fuss," he snapped, but started off anyway. Rust dropped the knives into the basket and Ma the shells.

"Come on, son."

He stood with the basket, aware quite suddenly that the sound from the waves was muting, their sharp tumble and crack becoming woolly, and he looked quickly to sea as the fog began to wisp over the Tambourine and the first clammy tendrils wafted stickily around the bare skin of his arms and legs.

"Gets his chest," Ma said as Pa coughed again. "Should have kept a closer watch on the sea and seen it sooner. Hurry."

As the three left the shadows of the cliffs, the rays of the sun stung them only momentarily before chilling as the heat was absorbed by the lacy, transparent curtains that drifted in like giant spiderwebs. The last sound from the waves faded away in a heavy thickness, and Pa was lost to sight somewhere ahead.

"His chest was bad last winter," Ma worried.

"Where'd y' put th' *Clinker?*" Pa's urgent shout came from the mists in the direction of the bar.

"The same place—"

"No it's not," Pa shouted back, and his muffled voice had an edge of anger to it.

"You go ahead and find it, son," Ma told the boy. "Quick!"

"You didn't pull 'er up," Pa snarled when Rust reached him. "She's gone off!" Ghost curtains wound about them, and Rust looked around in panic.

"That was a bit stupid, son," Pa rasped, trying to hide his anger. He began to cough again.

"Alfred, keep your coat tight about your chest," Ma panted as she appeared from the mists. "Where is she?"

Rust searched with desperate eyes, and caught sight of the boat's vague outlines deep in the mists across the Inlet. "There!" He stripped off his T-shirt.

"Rust!" Ma cried out as he ran out into the water. "We can walk round and come back for her when it clears." But Rust ignored her, Pa's cough driving him on, and threw himself forward and began to swim. By the time Pa managed the walk all the way round the edge, he'd probably be ill enough to go to bed.

He trod water to check his direction and resumed swimming. She didn't seem to have moved; she must have gone off the bar before the fog, while there was still a breeze. Yet he was *sure* he had pulled her well up. And then he remembered the noises in the house. His panic, together with the dull sound of his own arm-strokes in the fog, brought back the fear and he sucked water and spluttered and lost speed, choking, his eyes blurring, lost. . . He lifted his head and trod water again, fighting the panic; unable to find the *Clinker* in the mists. . .

Pa coughed, but not behind him; to the side. So Rust stroked himself round until that sound *was* behind. And there he found the *Clinker* at last, almost with a sense of surprise. Sucking in a deep breath, he swam, holding the air until the fingers of one hand scraped against her hull and he could grab her gunwale. He stopped there for a spell, resting, refilling his lungs, then lifted himself up and tipped over into the bottom of the boat.

Hurry!

He got to the seat and clattered the blades out of their resting-place and over the side, digging in and spinning the boat's head around for the bar, missing the water completely with the left oar and nearly going over backwards.

"I'm coming!" he cried, more for the sound of his own voice in the eerie stillness than to reassure Ma and Pa, for the fog now lay so heavily that his ears seemed packed with cottonwool.

He strained on the oars, rushed them back without heed of splashing water on the backstroke, and strained again, finding himself suddenly flat on his back with the oars standing out like the antennae of a probing ant.

"Good swim, son!" Ma's voice cried, and as he struggled upright she pushed the basket over the bow. "Come on, Alfred, hurry!"

Pa couldn't hurry: he was bent over in a spasm of coughing. Rust had time to leap out and pull the *Clinker* broadside to the sand before he reached them.

"Damned chest!" Pa wheezed, climbing unsteadily over the side. "*Blast* old age!"

"It was just the suddenness of the chill," Ma tried to reassure him.

"Hurry, Ma! I can push her off."

She climbed in over the side and Rust heaved the *Clinker* off the sand and tumbled aboard after her, spooking himself at the sound of a gull's mufflled *cark!* and missing his first stroke, the left oar clatting against the hull.

"Easy!" Pa snapped, and began coughing again, and Rust droped his eyes and pulled more carefully.

"Further right," Ma advised, peering. "I can't see, but I can feel we're too far down."

Pa tried to say something but yet another fit of coughing choked his words, and Rust concentrated on digging the blades deeply into the water.

"More right. I can see the outline of the bank trees."

"Have t' storm-tie 'er t'night," Pa managed.

"I'll attend to that with Rust."

"Don't want 'er gettin' off again."

"Pa! He wouldn't have left her drift on purpose."

Rust felt himself redden. Had he left her floating because of his panic?

"Steady," Ma called, but too late to stop the bow grounding with a suddenness that jerked Pa forward in his seat and almost overbalanced Rust again. "Sorry." He scrambled out and pulled her broadside to the bank, holding her there while they both climbed out.

"Straight up to the house Pa, and stir the fire!"

Rust lifted the oars onto the bank, pushed the *Clinker* out and tugged her on the painter to bring her round and out to the jetty, where he bent the line to the first ring.

"Here's the other line," Ma said behind him.

He took it and sat on the edge of the jetty and pulled the boat in with his feet, then dropped down into her and fixed the line to the ring in her stern. He reached up, secured the other end to the jetty ring and climbed out.

"I'll put them away, Ma," he called, seeing her lifting the oars. "You go in to Pa."

"You all right, son?"

"Yeah." He hurried out to the bank, got the oars and took them back to the locker, forcing himself to wait and wipe them down before he clattered them in, slammed the lid and ran. He could feel the mists on his legs as he hurtled into the mouth of the track in the tea-tree, and by the time he reached the lean-to outside the back door, he was breathless and panting.

"Rust," Ma said gently, taking her second boot off.

"It's just that I was running." He caught his breath, and tried to think of something normal to say. "The Tambourine would be dangerous to the old sailing-ships on a day like this, wouldn't it?"

"Not so bad. With the wind down they'd be lying becalmed. It was the storms drove them onto the reefs and shores. But don't talk about the Tambourine to Pa while the fog's down," she continued, picking up the basket and pausing by the door. "It preys on his mind, the *Ohio*."

"Is he sick, Ma?"

"No, but neither of us is young, son, and things we'd have once thrown off. . ." She shook her head and went through into the kitchen. Rust pushed the outside door closed behind him and followed her.

Pa was seated in front of the kitchen stove, the kettle set above the bright new flame he had built from the ashes.

"Go and change while I make us a cuppa, Alfred."

He shook his head. "Mist gets into th' house same as everywhere. Clothes in there would be just as damp, an' cold t' boot." He nodded towards Rust. "You better change, though: you got soaked. Storm-tie 'er?"

"We did," Ma said sharply.

Pa turned back to the open fire-door, nodding a little—but not quite with tiredness alone, Rust thought, and felt a sudden pain in his chest at the sight: Pa, an old, old man...

"I'll change." He went out to the hallway, but took only one step into his room before pulling back with a start. The brass lamp from the *Ohio* was on the floor, its glass broken, its bowl dented, kerosene in a pool across the floor. He looked up at the window. The half-light among the tea-tree seemed alive with ghostly shadows. Panicking, he turned and bolted back down the hallway.

"Rust!" Ma cried, startled by the anguish on his face.

"The lamp! In my room! It's on the floor, broken!"

Pa shoved himself to his feet and Rust stepped quickly aside as his great-grandfather stumped through.

"Rust...?" Ma moved towards him.

"Damn!" Pa thundered from up the hallway. "Y' left it too close t' th' edge!"

"I didn't, Pa," Rust cried, "I *didn't*!" He ran along the hallway as Pa disappeared into the room, and heard the crunch of boots grinding glass. "Pa?" The old man ignored him, and Rust turned desperately to Ma, right behind him. "I *didn't*! I loved that old lamp, truly!"

"It's all right, son," she comforted, putting an arm around him. "It's a troubled day." She hugged him. "Alfred..."

"Kitchen," he mumbled, pushing past them, the lamp in his hands.

"I'll get a broom and some rags," Ma said softly.

"I'll do it."

"We'll do it together. You can pick up the bigger pieces. Be careful."

He crouched down on his heels and lifted the largest piece, and began collecting the smaller bits into it. When had he heard it fall? *Before* the fog—he was sure it was before the fog. Nothing to do with the ghosts of sailors—that was stupid.

He glanced up at the twining tendrils of the fog, and shivered.

"I heard it fall, Ma," he whispered when she came back. "When I got the picnic. I was too spooked to go and see." He kept his eyes down, ashamed.

"Shhh. . . Get some clothes and go over to the bathroom and change while I clean this up."

He shivered again and pulled open a drawer, remembering, as he crossed the hallway, that he had not brought the cuttlebone Clinker up from the beach. He gritted his teeth. He couldn't go back for it, not in the fog. Not even if it meant the little carving might be blown or washed away.

He just couldn't.

Chapter Four

When Rust awoke the next morning he had a vague recollection of having had to get out of bed and remake it during the night, and of an odd dream of trying to catch the lamp as it fell from the chest of drawers and finding the *Clinker* in his hands instead. It had sort of been the cuttlebone *Clinker*, but then it had grown to full size and crushed him, him and Pa; because Pa had suddenly been there with him, gasping for breath. . .

Where would the closest doctor be? How would you get someone to hospital from here? If Pa had caught a chill yesterday. . . At his age he could probably *die* of it; and it would be his, Rust's, fault because he hadn't pulled the *Clinker* up far enough, or had kicked her off in his panic when he got out.

If only he could remember *exactly*. . .

He hugged the bedclothes to his shoulders, and kept his head still. The pillow was damp and cold where he hadn't been sleeping on it—*everything* was damp and cold. No wonder Ma was worried about Pa catching a chill. How did they manage to live in a house without heating?

And this was summer.

There was a sound from the kitchen. He had better get up and learn the worst. If only he could just go and have a hot shower, or even a bath; but the only hot water came from the chip heater at the bath's end, and he'd be *dead* from cold by the time he found wood and had it going.

Anyway, Pa had said the tanks were low and they'd have to conserve water till they had another rain. You didn't think of this sort of thing when you lived in a fully heated house.

He gripped a good handful of the bedclothes, stiffened his body, flung the blankets back and swung himself upright onto the floor. It was freezing! And something was sticking into the ball of his left foot.

He sat back heavily on the bed, crossed his left leg over his right and screwed his foot around. A tiny piece of glass. . . Shivering, he picked it out with the nails of his thumb and forefinger and waited for the blood; but it was such a minute little chip that it now seemed ridiculous it had even hurt.

He dropped the tiny fragment into the candle-saucer and rubbed the blood speck away, placing his feet more carefully this time and limping slightly towards the chest of drawers, his body shaking with cold. Mom would hardly approve, but he wasn't going to *touch* himself with water before he dressed. He was glad she had put in the jeans.

Sitting on the bed pulling his socks on, Rust glanced out the window, surprised at how blue and gold it was outside. The fog must be well gone. How long would the sun take to dry out the dampness?

"Shhh. . ." Ma warned as he came into the kitchen. She kissed him. "Pa's still in bed. He didn't have a very good night. I was just off down to the Robertses' to ask them to get me some more of Pa's cough syrup when they're in town today. Mrs Roberts slipped in for my list yesterday, but I never thought of the syrup." She shivered. "My, it got cold and damp last night." She added wood to the crackle of kindling in the firebox.

"I'll go down," Rust offered, reluctantly.

"Would you? You'd be much quicker. I'll write it down. You feed the fire up and warm your hands. I can't imagine what it must be like in Boston with a blizzard blowing."

"Cold," he said, adding wood, and feeling almost

ashamed at the thought of the warmth in his house back home, even in a blizzard, while Ma and Pa were cold after a mere summer fog.

"There." She handed him an envelope. "Money's inside."

He broke into a run as soon as he left the house, wanting to be out of the shadow of the tea-tree; but even the bright sun was not really warm yet, and he kept up his run along the sandy track and round to the other back door. Anne Roberts answered.

"Ma asked if you'd get some of this cough syrup for Pa in town today."

"The poor old man hasn't got that cough back again, has he? I thought he was going to die once last winter, but he wouldn't let us take him to hospital. I think we're going to have to force him if it happens again next year. Have your people ever thought of having them over there?"

Rust nodded, a lump rising in his throat at the thought of Pa so ill that he should be in hospital.

"But I don't suppose he'll go, will he?" she added.

"No. But we all want them over there."

"It'd be a lot to leave. I'll send Maggie straight over with this as soon as we get back. The bus doesn't get in till after four, though." She looked beyond him. "Here come Maggie and Bob now. Wait and say hello. We really love the music-box you gave her."

"I won't wait, Ma's getting breakfast."

He felt just like Maggie, the way he found himself turning and running, catching a brief flash of the girl and her father and their surfboards through the tea-tree as he went. He sprinted out to the front track, back along the line of dry footprints he had broken through the damp sand on his way there. Worse than Maggie, to flee like this. But he didn't turn back.

"*Now* you look warmer," Ma greeted him. "Porridge and toast?"

"Just toast," he panted. "Have you been back in to see Pa?"

"He's not specially bad, son. I just don't want it to settle on his chest."

"Mrs Roberts said he was really sick last winter."

She sighed. "We're not young, Rust. But we don't want coddling, either."

"You *should* come over and live with us."

She sighed again. "Perhaps. And perhaps it's best to stay amongst the old ways at our age. I don't know." Her eyes sparkled. "I've never *been* old before!" She stepped forward and hugged him. "Make the toast, it's all cut ready. You're here on a holiday! Pa'll be up again tomorrow and rarin' to go."

Rust went to the stove and poked the wood around, the way Pa did, till he had a bank of bright coals. He speared the first slice of bread.

"Why don't you take some lunch and go down to the end of the beach today? I wish you were friends with Maggie. It'd be nicer with two."

"I don't really want to go today, Ma."

"Well, that's fine. We'll find something to do."

"Could I put the new hinges on the gate?"

"That's a good idea. I'm just going to slip in and see if Pa's ready for some breakfast."

Rust stood the first slice of toast on the side of the stove to keep it warm and started another, breathing deeply the scents from the wood and the toasting bread, his mind slipping back to the brief sight of Maggie and her father through the trees. He envied them. The cold wouldn't matter if he was out surfing.

Ma returned. "He's ready, and he's promised to stay in bed for the day. Why don't you go in and keep him company while I get breakfast? He'd like that."

Rust hid his reluctance and handed over the fork. He had planned what he was going to say to Pa about yesterday, but he didn't relish the prospect of saying it.

"G'day, son."

"Good morning, Pa." He rushed on quickly. "I must have let the *Clinker* go adrift yesterday. I must have pushed her back when I jumped out. And . . . and I must have set the lamp too close to the edge." He shrugged. "I'm sorry."

Pa reached out a hand and gripped his forearm, and Rust felt a shock of fear run through him at the way Pa's hand trembled. "Sit down on th' bed, son. I've been thinkin' about th' *Clinker* goin' off yesterday, an' th' lamp. Reckon it might'a been th' sailors."

"The sailors?"

"Th' ghosts of 'em."

Rust wanted to pull his arm away, frightened of the glint in his great-grandfather's eyes; eyes that were looking at him but, he was almost sure, not really seeing him. Looking through, *beyond* him.

"But I probably did kick the *Clinker* off, Pa. When I jumped out. I was—spooked." He tried to bite the word back, but it was too late.

"Spooks. Ghosts. All th' same thing."

"I didn't mean it like that."

"An' th' lamp. Boy like you wouldn't be careless with it. Brrr . . . Damp in 'ere. Need a fire." He frowned, puzzled about something, and his eyes came back and focused. "How're you goin' t' spend th' day?"

"I thought I'd try and put the new hinges on the gate." Rust clutched at his great-grandfather's sudden return to something everyday.

"Might be a bit hard t' move th' old screws. Probably be easier t' hacksaw 'em off. There's tools in th' shed, though th' blades'll be a bit old an' rusty. Can't keep th' rust off 'em. There's a tin of lard on th' bench. Rub a bit of that on before you use it."

"I'd like to try." He turned his head slightly at the

sound of a woman's voice, younger than Ma's, from somewhere in the house. Mrs Roberts?

"Brrr . . . How about settin' me a fire in 'ere?"

"Sure," Rust agreed quickly, pulling his arm away. "I'll go and get wood now, Pa." He almost ran from the door, then stopped in the hallway. That other voice was still there. He wasn't going in till she'd gone, whoever it was.

He leaned against the wall, listening to the voices but thinking of Pa. And of the ghosts of the sailors. Pa seemed too big a man, too *strong* a man, to believe in spirits. He probably didn't really; it was just that he wasn't well. A fever could make you imagine all kinds of strange things. . .

"Thank you, Anne," Ma's voice concluded. "I don't know what we'd do without you and Bob and Maggie."

The back door closed, and Rust waited a moment before he went into the kitchen. "Pa wants me to light a fire in his room," he told Ma.

"I was just bringing a shovel of coals from the stove to start it when Anne came. They're on their way to the bus now. Why don't you go and get an armful of wood?"

By the time he came back with it Ma had fresh coals under kindling that crackled merrily in the bedroom fireplace, and Rust knelt down with his load and fed in larger wood. When Pa finally spoke he sounded quite normal again, and Rust felt the relief as a physical sensation running through him.

"Nothin' in th' world quite like a fire in th' room when you're not feelin' th' best. Don't usually need it in th' middle of summer, though."

"Breakfast!" Ma announced. She bedded a tray on a cushion across Pa's knees. "Will you go and bring ours, Rust? You and I can camp by the fire at the master's feet."

"Huh!" Pa snorted.

After breakfast Ma spread out on the kitchen table all the shells they had collected, and they sorted through them.

"We want only perfect ones for your mum," she remarked. Her fingers darted in and picked out one to study, a frown of concentration on her forehead. "Mm. I've been gathering them for sixty years and I'm still finding new varieties and variations."

"Is that a new sort?"

"I'm not sure. We'll get the book out tonight. I've marked every one I've found so far. The shells along this part of the coast are unique to here and Tasmania. There are so many—and probably even more just waiting to be discovered."

"Nellie!" Pa's call from the bedroom was gruff, but he sounded more like himself again.

"There goes my boy! His resting in bed is my wearing my feet out. Leave the shells there and we'll work on them through the day. You'll want to get on with your repairs."

"'K." Rust felt happier—and ashamed that he was glad Pa was not going to be around for the day, but glad anyway. He pulled open the back door, then remembered and turned back in sudden dismay. "Ma, did you pack the little cuttlebone *Clinker* Pa made on the beach?"

There was a moment's silence. "No. No, I didn't in all the rush."

"I'll go down and get it now."

"All right."

He pulled the door and sprinted down the path through the tea-tree and out onto the bank, giving a shout of surprise when a great white sticky-legged bird flapped away from the water's edge in front of him. He stopped and laughed and watched it go slowly away up the Inlet, gaining height as it went on wingbeats that settled from panic into steady pulsing thrusts, its legs trailing, the bill on its long neck pointing. An egret? Probably.

He broke into a gallop along the bank, frisking and leaping over tussocks until his legs tired and he jumped from the bank onto the sandy beach and jogged on along it under the cliffs, not even noticing Shaun and Tony out on the bar till he was nearly there and heard the music from their player.

But they ignored him, concentrating on pitching rocks out into the water.

He kept his eyes averted and ran on.

"Bombs away!" Shaun yelled.

"Good one!"

Rust glanced sideways, tripped and almost fell flat on his face as he spun around. "That's mine!" he shouted. "Don't. . .!"

But Tony ignored him and threw. Rust splashed desperately into the shallows, reaching out for the little white craft bobbing over the ridges of the earlier stones just as Tony's rock landed.

"Mine. . ." Rust choked as the tiny craft disappeared. The water climbed up into a ragged trumpet shape, then split and fell back, and the chips of the little cuttlebone *Clinker* rose in a scattered circle. "Pa made it for me!"

"Little boy lost 'is 'ittle boaty!" Tony jeered.

Rust reached out to gather the pieces in, but soon let his hands drop to his sides. The little carving was smashed beyond repair.

He turned for the bank on an angle, so that he wouldn't have to face them, and trudged back along the beach and up onto the grass of the home bank.

"Morning," Mr Taylor called from his deck as he passed. "Getting to know Shaun and Tony, eh? Don't let the old man put you off them." Rust felt compelled to acknowledge the greeting, so he lifted his hand briefly and went on. *Getting* to know them!

He went up through the tea-tree and slipped quickly into the shed, not wanting Ma to see him and ask if he'd found the carving; not right now anyway.

Pa had his tools set at the back of a wide bench, and Rust took a screwdriver, a hammer and a pair of pliers, and decided he had better take a hacksaw too. He unhooked the saw and tested the blade with his fingers. Fine-toothed—that should be right for steel. He looked for the tin Pa had mentioned, and rubbed lard along the blade to stop it jamming.

Cautiously he went to the door and looked out. He didn't even want to talk to Ma right away. But she wasn't in sight. He slipped out and ran down the side of the house to the gate.

The screws were so rusted that the blade of the driver refused to sit in the slots, no matter how hard he leaned into it, and after a moment he sat back on his heels, dispirited. Even cutting them off with the hacksaw wouldn't be easy, and was probably going to make the job look messy too.

But he had to try.

So he squatted down outside the gate and set the blade at the top of the hinge, sawing down between it and the wood of the post until he reached the first screw. It wasn't that the job was a hard one; but then it wasn't the job which was dispiriting him, it was Pa—or perhaps Pa and Ma. He had never thought of them as *old* old. And what about Pa going off about ghosts the way he had, even if he *was* ill, and getting that cough, that fever, so quickly from just a sharp change in the weather. Ma was certainly worried about it, and so was Mrs Roberts.

"You better wear this," Ma said, appearing with an old floppy straw hat. "Sun's hot even if the wind is cold, and just sitting in it's no good for the back of your neck. Been paddling?" she added, noticing his wet jeans.

"I . . . ran through the Inlet near the bar."

"You find it?"

He shook his head.

"Gone? There wasn't enough wind to move it, and the tide wouldn't have come that high." She huffed suddenly. "One of those holiday people must have taken it. You used to be able to leave a diamond brooch on the beach for a week without worrying about it."

Rust put the hat on, relieved that Ma had gone on with her own thoughts about the fate of the little cuttlebone *Clinker* and not questioned him.

"We'll get Pa to carve you another." She huffed again, this time in the form of a short laugh. "Not today though. I know who'd be cleaning up the bits and pieces in the bed! Don't worry if you can't get that job done. Pa'll help you tomorrow."

"I want to try."

"Just like all the rest of the Stewarts," she smiled— proudly, he realized—and bent and picked several pink-and-white pelargoniums from beside the path. "Brighten up the room for him."

Rust went back to sawing, concentrating fiercely to keep his mind from wandering, not sure whether to be relieved or not that Pa was no longer blaming him for everything.

"Look, honey: Huck Finn!"

His head snapped round and he gaped at the woman leaning from the car window. He had not even heard the car arrive, and for an instant the twanging Texas accent accelerated his mind into a dizzy spin, as though he had just been involved in an accident, or was emerging out of a dream; and he couldn't tell, in that instant, whether Sealers Inlet or the American accent was the dream . . .

"Can we take your picture, Huck? C'mon, be a honey."

She was already out of the car, and a man was clambering from the other side, fighting a video camera whose straps seemed to have developed an affectionate attachment for the vehicle.

"Abner, c'mon!" the woman cried back, not taking her eyes from Rust. "Just don't *move*, honey."

Rust lowered his gaze and began sawing again, hoping they would hurry up and be on their way.

"Hey kid, big smile for the camera, hey?"

Rust turned reluctantly. The man was moving the

camera sideways and up and down as though painting a picture of him. "Right on!"

The woman reached back into the car, withdrew a purse and took out a five-dollar bill. "There y' are, honey! Buy yerself somethin' nice."

Rust shook his head violently.

"Go'won, we're from America. Texas!"

"So am I," Rust managed. "Massachusetts."

The woman took a quick pace backwards, stumbled in the sand, and grabbed for the man to steady herself. "My Gard! What are you doin' *here* then?" Her face lit up. "You in the Peace Corps?"

"He's way too young."

"My great-grandparents live here."

"Aw, honey—you're findin' yo roots!" She was delighted, and turned to the man. "That's what *I* want to do, Abner, I wanna find my roots."

The man looked at his watch. "So we go to Italy after dinner."

Her face darkened at his sarcasm. "Irėland, Abner."

Rust jerked to his feet and bolted, suddenly hatless, past the side of the house and to the back, his hand almost on the doorknob before he changed his mind and shot off down the track through the tea-tree. If she was going to follow him to the house, he didn't want to be there.

He burst from the tea-tree and across to the locker, snatching out a pair of oars and running onto the jetty. He wished they hadn't had to storm-tie the *Clinker* last night. Two knots to undo instead of one.

He got the knots free and pushed off, dropping to the seat and fitting the oars, and was halfway across to the dunes when he saw the couple again. They had found their way to the bank, and the man was pointing the video camera at him. Rust felt angry, knowing they would have a zoom lens and could capture him on tape like trappers and take him back to America as though in a cage to show him to their friends. They might even be the kind who would try to sell the tape to some television news show. And there was nothing he could do about it but pretend he didn't know he was being taped and row as quickly as he could.

He bumped the bow of the *Clinker* hard up onto the narrow beach at the feet of the dunes and tumbled out on the sand, lashing the painter around a protruding root and scrambling off into safe secrecy under the low dark dune-trees, where he stopped and looked back through the break in the branches.

They were still pointing the camera, and he had a sudden creepy feeling that with a good enough lens they could probably probe right between the leaves and branches and record him crouching here like some strange beast frightened of humans. So he hunted round in the sand to pretend he was not hiding at all, and worked his way up the side of the dune, keeping behind as much cover as he could, but not really feeling safe until he had clambered over the humped top and rolled down the other side into a small hollow.

If he ever did go to some other planet, he'd never, *never*, treat any half-intelligent life in this manner — it was horrible. In fact, he'd remember this even when he was just a tourist somewhere.

He looked down to the ocean: not as calm as yesterday, the swells even but bigger, rolling in long, long lines that stretched off into the haze to the right and beyond the point to the left.

The tide was low and the Tambourine plainly visible, shreds of white water in the deep-blue of the sea. On the beach to his right two fishermen, probably the same ones he had seen before, were standing on the edge of the tide with surf-fishing rods.

He glanced back up to the ridge, almost as if expecting the video camera to have some kind of beam bending over the top of the dune. He leapt to his feet and went down in huge strides that took him out into space and dropped him in great steps down the sand until he was on the beach itself.

The craypot! He'd forgotten all about it. But he had promised not to go out on the rocks by himself. Perhaps the fishermen would be willing to keep an eye on him if he asked.

He ran along the hard to where they stood, like sentries with their tall rods, gazing along dipping lines of plastic thread that lifted and fell to the rhythm of the sea. Sentries from a distance, anyway; closer up, more like housepainters taking a break, judging by the look of the paint-spattered coveralls and equally marked sneakers that they wore.

"Hi," Rust called out, aware of sounding far more jovial than he felt. "Any bites?"

"G'day," responded the tall, red-headed one. "Pulled a couple of salmon." He nodded first to the basket, then to a spot beside it. "And that ray there."

The boy approached and crouched over the small banjo-shaped stingray, green-grey on top, its eyes on the flat on each side of the raised section that he guessed was its backbone and nose—if they had noses.

"Good eatin', mate," winked the other, short and kind of roly-poly with tangled black hair and bright amused eyes. "You can have him."

Rust felt his stomach churn.

"Me too," the same man laughed, his great bulging belly shaking. "Dunno why, 'cause I know they taste pretty good."

"I think it's the shape." Rust stood up. "My name's Rust Stewart. I'm staying with my great-grandparents over on the bank on the other side of the Inlet."

"Saw ya with a couple of old folk yesterday," the chubby one grinned. "Must have been them." He straightened up. "I'm Olly, and this great tall streak'a misery's Blue, would ya believe!"

"G'day, Rust," said Blue. "We're camped back of the dunes for a few days. Don't spread it around, though. Greenies are gettin' a bit strange about that kind of thing."

"They're like that at home too."

"Which is America," Olly grinned.

Rust nodded. "We put a crayfish pot down in the rocks yesterday, but I'm not allowed to go out on the shelf unless there's someone else about. I was wondering if you'd just watch from here while I went and got it."

"Come with ya," Olly said. "See what y' got. Don't want the ray?"

"Uh, no thanks."

The two men reeled their long lines in.

"We'll drop a hook off the edge of the shelf and see what's lurkin' there," Blue said as they walked. "Don't know what's the best bait for the rock fish, do you?"

"My father and grandfather said they used to get red meat out of something they called seacows. They grow on the rocks and squirt water if you press them."

"Oh yeh, I know 'em. Cunjevoi," Olly chimed in. "Where's the pot?"

Rust led them across the shelf, not remembering the exact spot until he saw the rope tied into the natural eyelet in the rock. He crouched down on the edge of the hole and looked in. "We've got three!"

"Beauty!" Olly chortled. "Let's get 'em up." He reached for the rope, hauled the pot to the surface and lifted it, dripping, onto the shelf.

One of the crayfish was quite small, but the other two were as long as Rust's forearm, scrabbling back and forth over the smaller one as they searched for a way out.

"Going to throw the little'un back?" Blue asked.

Rust nodded. "And you can have one of the big ones."

"Y' don't owe us, mate."

"We couldn't eat more than one," Rust insisted. "I'd just throw it back too."

"Now that *would* be a shame," Olly agreed. "Uh, how do you go about actually extractin' 'em?"

They sat on their heels and studied the pot. Suddenly they looked at each other and all three grinned at the same time.

"Toss a coin?" Blue suggested.

"Oh well, y' can only die once." Olly plunged his arm in and grabbed the smallest. "I'd hate to have t' pull out a lobster. Imagine the nippers on one of those!" He dropped the crayfish into the water, pausing to watch it snap away with violent movements of its tail, then put his hand back in.

Blue opened the top of the creel and Olly pushed the second crayfish quickly inside, jerking his hand back as he released it.

"I reckon the human race is goin' soft," Blue observed. "Won't eat good ray because the stomach heaves; half terrified of a cray . . . C'mon, Oll, young Rust doesn't want that stone left in there. Pot's the only way I can see of him carryin' his cray home." He waited. "Well? Ya don't reckon *I'm* gonna take the stone out, do ya?"

Olly's stomach shook with low laughter. He reached in and snatched the anchor-rock from the bottom, and Rust took it and put it back in the hole where Ma kept it.

"An' now f'r a bit of bait," Olly said, hacking the top from the warty brown-green cone of a cunjevoi attached to the shelf and exposing bright-red meat. "Looks like pretty good tucker."

"Thanks for helping me." Rust fed the rope into the pot.

"She's right. See ya, mate."

He carried the pot back across the shelf and the beach to the foot of the dune, and by the time he reached the top he was on his knees pushing it ahead of him. He got to his feet and plunged down the other side, slipping near the bottom and tumbling down onto the beach, the crayfish clacking in panic as it rolled right into the water.

"Come back here!" he shouted, suddenly joyful. He manoeuvred it into the *Clinker* and pushed off, the boat skimming the water as he half-stood for each stroke, feeling the skin at the corners of his mouth stretched by his grin. He had forgotten all about the couple with the camera.

He glanced quickly behind to check his way and saw Ma seated on the locker. She waved and he dropped an oar to wave back before heaving again, urgent to show her the catch. "We got three crays," he shouted as he came into the jetty and stood to reach out and bring the *Clinker* alongside. "There were two men fishing down there and they helped me get the pot." He handed her the painter as she walked out, and pushed the oars up onto the jetty decking. "One was small, so we put him back, and I gave the other big one to the fishermen."

"Mm, he'll make a nice salad lunch tomorrow," Ma said as he lifted the pot up after the oars.

"I'll just dry the oars and put them away. How's Pa?"

"He's asleep. I've had visitors—I believe they met you out at the gate."

"Oh, those two Americans. Gee, did they come and see you?"

"*And* took my photograph! They said they filmed you out on the Inlet and wanted to add me to it. They're going to send a copy to your mother and father when they get back."

Rust dried the oars and put them away, hoping that his anger while they were taping—his panic, really—wouldn't show too much. He picked up the pot, and found Ma's arm suddenly linked with his. "It's so wonderful having you over here with us, son."

He smiled.

"Like a dream come true," she continued, releasing his arm so that they could walk single-file through the tea-tree tunnel. "They're going to have to civilize you all over again when they get you home." She stopped at the shed.

"I'll take the cray in while you pour a bucket of fresh water through the pot to clear the salt."

Rust was impressed by the quick, confident way in which Ma plucked the crayfish out of the pot, recalling how he and the two fishermen had debated whose fingers should be risked.

"Oh," Ma said, stopping halfway to the house. "I got out another lamp for you. It needs filling, so bring up the kerosene when you come and we'll fill up the fridge too. It's been working overtime with all the heat we've had."

"'K." He searched out a bucket and whistled his way round to the tank with it. When he went in, there was a glass of milk on the table, with a slice of fresh bread that Ma had baked. The kettle on the stove was just beginning to steam.

"Pa's still asleep," she motioned. "I'll show you how to fill the fridge, then we'll have a little smackerel of something."

He laughed at Pooh's words coming from her mouth, and they tipped kerosene into the reservoir that fed the refrigerator's wick, and filled the glass bowl of the rose-patterned lamp.

"Do you think they'll bring electricity in, Ma?"

She sniffed. "Bound to. These holidaymakers aren't getting *away* from it all; they're bringing it all with them!"

"It'll be easier for you, though. You'll be able to get a blender, and a hot-water service, and heaters." He frowned, remembering the wood-fired copper in the back laundry. "And a washing-machine."

"Ha! Then I'll be able to go away and die somewhere and the house will keep on running without even knowing I'm gone." She laughed all of a sudden, and hugged him. "I'd miss the smell of wood fires and kerosene lamps too much."

Rust took the kerosene back to the shed, washed his hands under the tap at the tank and went back in to the kitchen.

They were just finishing their morning tea, sorting the shells still spread on the table, when there was a knock at the door.

"Hello?" Bob Roberts poked his head around.

"Come in, Bob. Just in time for a cuppa."

"Ah, no thanks, Mrs Stewart. Just had to slip home for a new chain for the saw. Noticed the tools round the gate and picked up a brace with a screwdriver bit I thought Rust might find useful."

"Oh, thanks."

"Got a moment to come out? I'll show you how it works."

"Take your hat," Ma said. "The Americans brought it in."

Rust followed out to the gate. "Probably sawing the way you're doing is best. Actually wanted a quiet word with you," Bob said. "There's the brace." He squatted down by the gatepost but made no attempt to pick it up. "Anne and I've been worried about your great-grand-parents for a year or so now. They've been really good to us, letting us rent their other place for nearly nothing when we arrived a few years back. It was your Pa got me the job with the Forests Commission." He indicated the utility with the FOREST RANGER sign on the cabin. "Think there's any chance of persuading them to go over to the States to live?"

Rust shrugged. He didn't want to have to work out such things.

"Listen, I know it's a bit much to put on you, Rust. But when you get back home I think you ought to tell them over there that Mr Stewart *is* getting a bit frail. Anne thought that cough he had last year was going to turn into pneumonia—and he wouldn't let us take him into hospital."

"I don't know . . ." Rust said helplessly.

"Just wanted you to know so you can tell them. Anne

and Maggie and I will do everything we can to see they're all right, but it's not the same as their own family."

"I'll tell Mom and Dad."

"Good. And I'd like to see you and Maggie friends before you go. You surf?"

"Sure."

"I'll work on her." He stood up. "Better get back to it. Just thought I'd snatch the chance while I had it. Got to get you out in the bush for a day before you go, though. Don't forget that."

"Thanks."

Rust remained squatting by the gate until the utility had crossed the blacktop of the highway and disappeared along the back road. He sighed and walked back by the side of the house. It wasn't like the holiday he had planned.

He stopped just back from the window. Ma was still at the table, one hand holding a shell. But it wasn't the shell she seemed to be looking at, and her face didn't have its usual brightness. It was sort of shrunken; almost. . . *collapsed.*

Rust ducked and ran below the sill so that she wouldn't see him, remembering his father's prescription for this kind of feeling, this despair that seemed to drag down his whole body. He repeated the old formula voicelessly to himself: *Go sailing. It mightn't solve your problems, but it'll sure clear your mind.*

He got the sailing gear from the locker and stacked it on the jetty, tossing his hat down into the boat. But suddenly fearful that Ma might come looking for him and see his despair, he tumbled all the gear in next to the hat, stepped the mast and climbed over the side, untying the painter and working the *Clinker* out to the end of the jetty before shoving away.

He did not even wait to fit the boom then, but ran the sail and pulled it back by hand, using it to scoop the wind and send the *Clinker* running, free of the land and everyone on it, wishing he was heading out through the break in the bar for the horizon...

He let the sail flap out and fitted the boom and rudder, then tied the sail back and pushed the port leeboard down.

Now he'd be able to test Dad's theory.

He tightened the mainsheet to the limit and brought her head closer to the wind, holding her there till her port gunwale was hissing crystal-white spray—and everything went from his mind but the need to hold her just there, because one more centimetre, one slight lapse of concentration and the gunwale would go under, the sudden rush of water instantly turning the *Clinker* from a beauty into a beast, a sloppy barge of a thing until he bailed her.

He ran her on that long-reaching tack leg until she was almost on the swamp mud, and then eased her off and around, tangling himself in the complications of changing the leeboards over, the mainsheet round his neck at one stage before he was able to set the new tack. No wonder someone had invented the centreboard! He chose a point down under the dunes to see how exactly he could keep her on a line, using only the mainsheet for control, the tiller absolutely still.

A half-smile of concentration tugged at the corners of Rust's mouth. It was almost impossible not to move the tiller—as in those tests where you tried to pat your head with one hand while rubbing your stomach in a circular motion with the other. He found himself resisting an urgent desire to correct with the tiller, had to jam it against his hip to stop himself, and ended breathless and laughing way offshore from the mark. He let the sail go flapping away as he brought her round, exhausted by the concentration.

Dad was right!

He snatched in the main as a brilliant white spoonbill coasted out of the sky for a long run down the airway of the Inlet. He set the *Clinker* out after it, trying to keep the point of the mast along the line of the spoonbill's flight. But the bird, without apparently moving a feather, planed down into the wind and was on the sand of the bar so long before the *Clinker* had even reached the lower edges of the swamp that Rust called no-contest and eased the main away.

This was what he would do every day: sail, fair wind or foul, until he became so expert that there would be nothing he could not do with her.

He waved vigorously as Ma came down the bank, watching to see if she would signal that she wanted him. But she just waved back, went to the locker and sat down, so he brought the boat closer to the wind to make her heel and leave a white track, knowing he was showing off and knowing Ma would know it too, and that he was doing it for her.

He'd go down to the bar, and come back really surging on the ocean wind funnelled in by the cliffs and the dunes on either side. He jibed and swapped leeboards as he approached the bar, laughing aloud as the spoonbill tumbled back into the air in surprise, gasping as the hard breeze from the opening almost put him over.

"Hey!" The word jerked out of him as he fought to regain control, spray coming over the gunwale and sloshing into his face, leaving him gasping. "Wow. . .!"

He got her running even before he had sorted out the tangle, panting and laughing at the same time at her speed, his whole body alive with the zinging excitement that vibrated through the very timbers of his craft.

And then he caught sight of Shaun and Tony on their deck, falling about with exaggerated mocking laughter, and he eased the sheet and spilled the wind and turned her head for the jetty, the spirit gone out of him.

Chapter Five

He was the first awake again the next morning, but even the brightness of the early sun outside his window could not tempt him to get up, and he rolled over and pulled the bedclothes up round his ears.

Ma had seen the two boys laughing at him from their deck yesterday, and had understood why he had come in. But you couldn't let other people steal time from you by allowing them to eat into your mind, she had told him. That's what it was, she had said, stealing; and time was precious.

Rust sighed. He knew what she meant; but it wasn't easy to stop it happening, to switch off your thoughts and feelings, just like that.

He turned the bedclothes back, got up and went to the window, removing the screen so that he could lean on the sill and breathe in the scents of the leaves and the earth and the salt on the breeze: the special smell that Dad said you'd never forget.

He sighed again. Dad would be mad if he knew how he was letting everything get to him like this.

Pulling his clothes from the bed, he dressed and climbed out the window, wondering what Pa would be like today. Up and wanting to do things? Or . . . Sharply he cut off the thought and broke into a run, not even bothering to detour for a fresh strawberry, straight into the entrance of the tea-tree track. He ignored the scatter of rabbits, but glanced quickly towards the Taylors' house before scuffing his way down to the gear locker at the head of the jetty.

It was easier to step the mast while she was still afloat, using the height of the jetty to drop that spar down into its hole. He drew her into the bank to complete the setting up, tossed in a life-jacket, and tied the painter with several large knots just in case the Taylor kid or his dumb friend got up early, which he doubted. . .

He spun round abruptly at the sound of movement in the bushes.

"G'day, Rusty," Olly chortled, plonking himself down on the locker and dumping creel and rods. "Phew! Just about ready to go back to work for a holiday! Off crayin'? Best feed I've had in a long while."

"I might be able to use the gun again tomorrow morning. We need rabbit for bait."

"That *you* bangin' away the other day, was it? Thought the greenies might have been after me and Blue. One with each barrel?"

Rust shrugged, embarrassed. "It was my first try. The second one was an accident."

"Old double-barrel with two triggers, eh? Might tell you the story of *my* first go with one of them some day." He shook with laughter as he got to his feet. "Ah, well, might wander round and see if there's anything doin' off the rocks. That cungy was good stuff. Catch you around."

"See you."

Olly went on along the bank, breaking into a yodel which sounded so blissfully contented that Rust found himself smiling, and leaping exuberantly for one of the higher branches as he went back through the tea-tree. When he emerged, still sprinting, at the other end, Ma was there. She had just gathered an armful of wood.

"I'll take that, Ma." Rust took the wood from her and followed into the kitchen, loading it into the woodbox by the stove. He should have thought to check the supply before leaving.

"Pa's feeling fine, today. He's dressing now."

"Swell. Will I start the toast?"

She sliced bread while the boy raked a pile of coals in the fire. He pulled up a chair and pronged the first piece.

"Mornin', son."

"Morning, Pa." Rust turned his head and flashed a grin in response to the sound of vitality in his great-grandfather's voice. "I've been down and rigged the *Clinker* ready to sail."

"Good idea. Want t' make th' most of this kind of weather. I'll come down an' drop a line off th' end of th' jetty f' company."

There was a knock at the door. "Who is it?" Ma called, turning.

"I've brought the milk, Ma."

Ma hesitated. Rust looked towards her, not noticing the toast move into the coals.

"Well, come on in," Pa rumbled. "Never known you to stand out there, Maggie."

But even Pa paused then, all of them waiting. She came in, her eyes averted, almost succeeding in hiding her face behind her long blond hair by the way she held her head.

"Thank you, dear." Ma took the billy. "Have you met Rust properly yet?"

She shook her head, and Rust got clumsily to his feet, knocking the slice of toast off the fork. "Uh—" He bent and picked it up. "Ouch!" he winced as he dropped it on the side of the stove, feeling his face flushing hot with embarrassment. "Hi."

"Hello. I'll have to go now, Ma."

"Stay an' have a glass of milk with us," Pa invited.

"Dad just told me I had to come in and say hello," she replied, and turned quickly for the door and disappeared.

"Well," Ma said softly, "that's a start. I better cut another slice."

"It's not badly burnt," Rust said quickly, glad not to have to say anything about the visit. "It's fine for me."

Maggie was suddenly back in the doorway. "Would

you like to come surfing with us one day?" she asked. They were all caught by surprise again; Maggie broke into a blush.

"Uh—oh, yeah," Rust managed after a moment.

"I'll tell Dad."

"Thanks."

"My," Ma whispered.

Rust sat down and began toasting another slice. Even if it was only because her father was making her, it would be better to have something to do with Maggie; and it would give him his chance to surf here.

"You surf much?" Pa asked.

"Whenever I can. I like skateboarding too."

Pa frowned. "Never 'eard of it. Seems t' me there's a lot I don't know about m' family these days."

"Why don't you both come and live in Boston?" Rust asked, snatching his opportunity. "Or somewhere near? Dad's always seeing little towns he thinks would be just right for you—places with lakes or small rivers."

"Nothin' t' stop 'em all from comin' back 'ere," Pa answered curtly. "They were th' ones that left."

"Alfred!"

Pa snorted. "Anyway, wouldn't *want* 'em back here with th' kind of people we're gettin' for holidays—and more houses planned, Bob says."

"It's only that we miss you," Rust said hurriedly to try to stop Pa fuming.

"Gettin' grizzly in me old age," Pa apologized. "Might carve y' out some oars for that little cuttlebone boat I made y', while I'm fishin'."

Rust cast a despairing look at his great-grandmother.

"Carve one that will last, from wood," she said. "Cuttlebone's only for playing around with. You know how they break, Alfred, no matter how careful you are."

The old man let himself down into his chair at the table, nodding. "Mm. Cut it out of that silky piece of foreign wood I made that little doll for Maggie with. Ha!

Maybe any of 'em still lost 'c'n go back t' America in 'er with you."

"Alfred! We've had enough of ghosts. Toast ready, son?"

"I think so." Rust checked the slice and pulled it off the fork. "I've burnt this one a bit, too."

"Good for the blood," Ma said. "Or the teeth, depending on who you're telling to eat it." She came to the stove for the kettle. "Let's not waste good sunshine sitting round inside."

She made Pa put on an extra jumper before he went out.

"Will I dig some worms for you?" Rust suggested.

"Mm. Might leave startin' that little boat for you till later. Want t' rough it out with a saw before I start carvin'."

Rust got the shovel and a can, and they went down to the vegetable garden. "Strawberry, Pa?"

"Ta."

He got one for himself too, and then dug the worms. "Can I try for another rabbit tomorrow, Pa?" he asked as he put the shovel away and followed along the track.

"Shoulder stand it?"

"It was more the surprise and the sunburn. I can't feel anything now. I'll only load one barrel though, just in case."

"Righto. Livin' well, aren't we, eh? Cray, bream, rabbit."

"We could have had ray too. The fishermen I met on the beach offered me one."

"Should have took it." Pa stopped at the bank by the jetty and looked with surprise at the heavily knotted painter. "You do that? Thought'n you could bend on a rope without all that tangle."

"Uh, I was talking to one of those fishermen while I did it," Rust mumbled, not wanting to get Pa stewing again by mentioning the real reason. Pa shook his head and went to the locker for his fishing-gear, which included an old cushion for the jetty. He carried it out to the jetty's end.

"Good stiff breeze for you out there. Let's see what you can do with it."

Rust ran back, worked the knots undone and pulled the *Clinker* out to the end of the jetty with his hands. "I'll go right up to the end, to the mouth of the creek."

"Be a hard job workin' her back against this breeze."

Rust grinned and pushed away, dropping a leeboard and tightening the mainsheet until the lee gunwale streamed white water.

It *was* hard working back, and Pa's shout of approval added to the sense of accomplishment. He didn't risk spoiling it by going as far down as the Taylors', but on his second run he noticed a truck unloading timber onto the low heath and tea-tree near their house; and he realized as he came down for the third time and saw the two boys climbing over the heap that they had lost interest in him for the moment, and he went on down as far as the bar, hoping he'd see Maggie.

Then Ma appeared on the jetty and Pa waved him in. She had brought a Thermos of tea and a bottle of stone ginger, and Rust caught hold of the side of the jetty and reached with his other hand for the glass Ma handed down.

"I planned on bringing lunch later," she said, "but the wind's too chilly."

"Don't you picnic on the inside of the dunes when there's a southerly?" he asked.

Ma smiled. "My, your father's filled you well up with local knowledge."

"Can we, then?"

Ma nodded. "All right. I'll go and make up a basket and we'll spend the afternoon."

"What's left of it," Pa said, looking west.

Ma reached for Rust's empty glass. "Then I'd better hurry."

"I'll get the mast down."

"No, we can sail," Ma said. "I haven't sailed for a long time."

When she came back they crossed to the sandy beach in the lee of the dunes, where they climbed out and settled themselves in the shade of a twisted dune tree with its dense, tough foliage. Rust was surprised by the heat reflected from the open patches of sand.

"Your grandfather talk of retirin' yet?" Pa asked, finding himself a comfortable seat on a low horizontal branch. "He's sixty-two this year. Only gives him three years, at most."

"There's no retiring age at home. Dad says that having good healthy brains going to waste is a luxury America can't afford. And Grandad wouldn't retire anyway. He tells us they're going to have to carry him out in a box with the lid nailed down! He gets really excited about chip storage instead of disks. He's been working on it for years and he says it's nearly here. Gran says it keeps him young."

Pa cleared his throat. "Don't even know what you're talkin' about." He sighed. "My mistake was goin' into a job where you needed body muscle instead of brain muscle. Haven't got much choice about retirin' then. Soon as your muscles go, you go."

"Now, Alfred—there was never much choice in our day. And you did well enough."

"Yeh. . . Yeh, s'pose I did." His head jerked up. "Confound it!"

"Alfred, they've every right . . ."

The blare of the tape-player grew quickly, and they realized that Shaun and Tony were running. Tony carried the player this time, while Shaun held a shiny—and, Rust guessed, new—air-rifle.

"Be careful where you go shootin' with that thing!" Pa called out as they ran past. But they kept their heads down and ignored him, and the sound of the music faded with them.

Ma leaned and patted Pa's knee, and Rust rolled over onto his stomach in the sand, digging with a finger to bring the grains pouring down in miniature avalanches, the sun soaking hot into his back.

After lunch he sailed again, using the bottom end of the Inlet most of the time, partly to avoid any contact with Shaun and Tony, who were hunting with the air-gun amongst the tea-tree at the top end, but mostly in the hope of seeing Maggie. He had a feeling she wouldn't be too hard to persuade to come out in the boat with him, and he knew how Ma and Pa would like that. But then rolling stormclouds stole the sun, Ma was waving for him to come back in to the beach, and he found that the freshening wind had wound its chill way even into the scalloped shelter of the dunes. And Pa was shivering. . .

The run home was a sizzling sprint with the wind broadside on, the bow slapping at the corrugations of the swells.

"Like *you* used to sail 'er, Nellie!" Pa whooped, his eyes sparkling. "Never could make 'er run like this m'self."

It occurred to Rust that he was being selfish. "You should have taken the helm, Ma. Will you, tomorrow, and let me crew?"

Ma seemed taken aback, but then nodded emphatically. "Yes, I will. I've had two other generations of Stewarts crew for me; why not the third?"

"Might have t' wait a few days," Pa warned, looking back to the west.

"A little rough weather never stopped me in the past," Ma retorted.

"Storm sailing would be great here." Rust was full of enthusiasm as he loosed the mainsheet and lifted the leeboard for the run up onto the mud.

"Well, you wear that life-jacket if it gets any brisker than this," Pa cautioned. He was shivering. "Come on, let's hurry this up an' get into some shelter."

"I'll fix everything, Pa. You and Ma go back. I'd like to do some more work on those hinges, too."

"Give you a hand. Be out of th' wind there, but I'll take up your offer an' go back an' warm up first."

Rust pulled the gear off the boat and lugged it back to the locker, wiping it all down before he stowed it. Then he pushed her off, walked her out along the jetty and tied her. As he finished he saw the swans coming in high above the bar, and he watched them make a wide circle before they entered their landing glide.

They were early. Was it a really big storm coming?

He watched their red feet and legs dropping like air-brakes, then like water-brakes splitting the surface in two brief tracks before the wide wings turned to become scoops that took off the last of their speed and folded with a shrugging ruffle as they settled into the water.

He turned and ran for the tea-tree track, hoping Shaun and Tony would leave the birds alone.

"Hot chocolate?" Ma greeted him as he came in. She poured steaming milk from a saucepan.

"Hope I've got a drill-bit small enough for th' new screws," Pa said, rubbing his hands in front of the open fire-door of the stove.

As soon as they had finished their drinks, Rust gathered up the hinges and carried them out to the gate with Pa. "I've still got to saw off the old ones. Bob lent me a screwdriver bit in a brace, but I haven't got enough weight to make it stay in the slots."

"Giv'us a try," Pa said.

He managed to budge some of them, Rust sawed off the rest, and together they replaced them with the black cast-metal hinges the boy had brought with him.

"An' she swings again!" Pa said, pleased. "I'm goin' t' have t' get t' work straightenin' up th' pickets an' paintin' 'em t' match."

"I can help. It's a good place to work when it's blowing."

"Right. Now, let's get in a good supply of wood an' have a fire in th' big room. Be a night t' snug down."

"And hear the ghosts from the *Ohio!*" Rust joked— but wished immediately that he hadn't as a shadow crossed the old man's face and his eyes seemed to drift away for a moment. "I'll get the wood," Rust added quickly. Collecting the tools and the old hinges, he ran with them back to the shed, his own words working on him as the stormclouds rolled and the sound of the surf lifted into thunder out beyond the bar. It was probably a night like this that had driven the American ship onto the Tambourine. He shivered, and dashed with an armful of wood and kindling to the house.

"Take it in an' I'll set her while you get some big stuff," Pa said, and by the time he came back the lounge-room had come alive with the leap and snap of dancing flames from the kindling. As the last of the day was lost behind the black stormbanks, Ma lit the Aladdin lamp and its mantle glowed red, then white with light. The rising wind was beginning to worry at the house, nipping and shaking it, playing drumrolls with loose boards, playing ghosts in the chimney . . .

"Ha!" Pa got up off his knees from the hearth and eased himself into his chair, listening. And Rust, taking his place on the hearth-rug, listened too.

"Now, now," Ma snapped, bringing in a tray and reading their faces. "You two'll frighten yourselves to death, sitting there silent and listening."

Rust tried to be busy rearranging the fire, and Pa snorted in indignation.

"Get yourself a patch of coals and start the toast, son," Ma ordered. "We'll have tea and then a game of Mono-poly. Your father always enjoyed that."

"Yeah," Rust responded, remembering. "He told me."

"Have to get used to Pa's way, though. Won't use money, so we have to let him keep his score on a pad."

"*Cheques*, to you," Pa said heartily, making an effort to brighten his mood for the sake of the boy. "Can't stand shufflin' playmoney about."

"Dad told me that too." Rust made a patch of glowing coals with the poker, took a toasting-fork from a hook in the brickwork and speared the first slice.

"We'll start while we're eating," Ma decided, putting a low table in front of the fire and Pa. She pulled the Monopoly set from inside the piano stool before going back to the kitchen for another tray.

"I've never seen a board with 'Mayfair' and 'Park Lane' on it. Ours has got American streets."

"Gives us th' home-ground advantage. Probably need it against a young brain, eh Nellie?"

"I think a little old-fashioned sense and experience might win the day," she disagreed. "My!" The room had lit up with lightning, and they all started at the intensity of the thunderclap that followed, the shockwaves from the superheated air shaking the whole house before rolling away into the ranges as the first rattle of rain echoed from the corrugated iron of the roof.

"You think t' storm-tie th' *Clinker*?" Pa asked.

"No. . ."

"Damn!" Pa mumbled, beginning to rise.

"One tie's enough to hold her, Alfred," Ma snapped in sudden irritation. "She's not going to break that rope in a month of Sundays!"

"I'll be back." The old man stood up.

"Come on then, Rust," Ma grumbled, motioning to Pa to sit down. "He won't settle till he knows it's done."

"You don't have to come, Ma," Rust said quickly.

"But I—"

"It's all right. I'll be quick." He couldn't let Ma go out in the storm. It was his fault—he should have thought. And Ma would probably catch something too if she went out now.

"Y' lines have t' be loose enough t' let 'er rest on th' mud if th' bar goes," Pa cautioned.

"I remember." Rust blinked as the lightning flared again. "Will I pull the drapes?"

"Uh, curtains? No. Like t' watch 'er."

"More than safe enough on *one* line," Ma huffed. "Get a coat from behind the back door."

"OK." Rust snatched an old coat from a nail behind the door, pushing his right hand way down the tunnel of the sleeve to reach the doorknob and staggering back as the door blew open against him.

He fought it closed from the outside against both the wind and the lino that bulged up with the wind, surprised by the darkness that had closed in. He felt hampered by the flapping of the coat around his legs and wished he had just made a dash without it.

Lightning flashed again, and Rust shivered as strange shapes darted and melted amongst the trunks of the tea-tree, and wished he had let Ma come too. He dropped his head and ran down past the shed and into the mouth of the track, a wind-tunnel now with the trees on the bank acting as wings to funnel the storm in.

The night lit up again, and he stumbled and had to stop and squeeze his eyes tightly shut to try to force the arc-like flashes from them. He thudded into a trunk as the batter of a thunderclap disoriented him, bringing with it sheeting rain that added more distortion to the night, and he stopped at the end of the track to get his bearings. It was then that he saw it—some wild flapping thing the height of a man, going by on the wind; and then another, and another . . .

If there were more he wasn't there to see them, for he was fleeing blindly back along the track with the wind adding speed to his panic. At last he slammed into the corner of the shed, grasped at it, felt his way frantically along the wall to its door and shoved it open.

What . . . what had they been? There was no such things as ghosts. . .

He crouched back against the tool-bench, terrified. What if they came for him here — because this bench too was made from the timbers of the *Ohio*. . .?

He bolted again, not waiting to pull the door, skidding in beneath the shelter of the lean-to and crouching down against the back door. He couldn't go in yet. They'd know he wouldn't have had time to put the storm-tie on and Ma would insist on coming out; and he'd have to come with her, but he wouldn't be able to. And after all, Ma *had* said that the *Clinker* would be all right on her painter.

Something crashed and scraped across the iron of the roof above him and Rust choked on a sob, and pressed closer to the door, tears taking the place of the rain — which had now stopped again. He began mewing like a castaway kitten, bitterly ashamed of it but helpless in the terror of the night.

"Mom. . .!"

A jag of lightning lit his eyes through the closed lids, and he cowered to wait for the thunderclap, which came almost at once, and jerked in a spasm of fear as the very concrete beneath his feet shook; and some nightbird cried out and he didn't know when its cry finished because he found himself crying out too, at the top of his voice, and felt himself raking at the door with his fingers in a desperate search for the knob; and he was dimly aware of the lino lifting again in the wind and jamming the door half open, and vividly conscious that his furious struggle with the door as he squeezed his way in was full of panic and of dread. . .

"Russell?"

"Huh!" Rust suppressed a sob as he backed against the door to slam it shut behind him.

"You *were* quick. Young legs!"

Panting, he disentangled himself from the coat, making

several attempts to hang it up before the nail snagged it.

"Your head's sopping! I'll get a towel. Straight up to the fire with you!"

Hail began to clatter on the roof as Rust went into the lounge-room, avoiding the uncurtained window and wishing Pa would let him draw the drapes.

"All shipshape?" Pa asked loudly against the noise of the hail. Rust managed a quick grin, so that he wouldn't have to tell Pa a lie, and knelt on the rug close to the fire.

"I'll give it a good rub," Ma said, bending and putting the towel over his head.

"Thanks." His spirits took a sudden leap at the wonderful everydayness of the towel over his head and of Ma's hands rubbing so briskly—just like Mom always did.

"There! I've got a saucepan of milk simmering on the stove for some cocoa, and then we'll get back to our game."

He sat back on his heels, aware that the clanging of the hailstones was melding now into the steady drum of heavy rain. He stirred the fire and added a log, hoping Pa wouldn't ask any direct questions and feeling suddenly foolish at letting himself be spooked like that. They were probably just broken branches being bowled along the bank—the wind was certainly strong enough. That was all they would have been. So. . . His mind shied away from what tried to follow: go back out now and put on the storm-tie. . .

He shook his head violently.

"Y' look like a dog," Pa growled. "You'd be throwin' water all over th' place if Ma hadn't dried y'." Rust managed a grin again, but inside he was desperate with shame. "*I* was just about to put houses on," Ma said. She placed the steaming drink on his plate and sat down again.

"Well, if you want t' win you better charge more rent than y' charge th' Robertses," Pa advised.

"They pay enough. It's not just money that counts."

Rust breathed in the warm steam, and sipped, aware that there had been no close flashes or thunderclaps for several minutes.

"Goin' back into th' ranges," Pa said. "Lot of water'll be comin' down t'night; that's why she had t' be storm-tied."

The rim of the mug clattered against Rust's teeth.

"Fill the tanks," Ma observed, pleased. "Your roll, Alfred."

He took the cylinder and tipped the dice onto the board. "Wish you could be back in th' bush with me when she comes down like this, son. After a good dry like we've had she just runs right off th' top at first. Gets t' chatterin' along in all th' little dips an' hollers till they reach the creeks, an' they start jumpin' t' bust! Time she gets down t' th' back bridges she's a banker an' carryin' fair-sized bits of tree. Then she slows right down as she goes over th' banks an' runs out across th' flats. That's why th' bottom land's so rich, why I held it back 'case you wanted t' try your hand on th' land. What do I owe you?"

His miniature flatiron had ended on Bond Street, and Ma read off the rent and collected the money directly from the bank while Pa made a subtraction from the balance on his pad.

"Will we see the flood in the morning?"

"Depends." Pa inclined his head to listen to the sound of the rain. "Will if th' bar can hold it back; but if she goes, there'll be nothin' but a little gutter of a creek out there tomorrow, an' th' stain of th' mud a mile out t' sea. Be able t' see it from th' dunes."

Rust rolled the dice, hoping Ma and Pa would think the shake in his hands was deliberate, a private way of trying to roll luck. If the bar did break, with the *Clinker* on just the one line...

He looked at the window, and looked away as the

reflections from the lamplight prickled off the spattering water on the pane. A sudden acceleration of the wind moaned in the chimney and pushed smoke back into the room.

"Damned thing!" Pa choked. "No comfort if she's goin' t' be one of *them* nights! Never could beat th' downdraft when th' wind went round due south. Kicks up over th' dunes an' drops right down." He leaned forward in a spasm of coughing as more smoke huffed out. "May as well give it away now an' go t' bed."

Rust snuggled under the eiderdown Ma had brought in and tried to pretend the gurgle in the gutters was one of the creeks in the bush. His mind kept bending back to the *Clinker*, and he couldn't shut out the vision of those flying—

"No!" He snarled the word out, thrust his face into the pillow, and dragged the covers up tightly against each side of his head. Tomorrow—when the storm had blown itself out—before Ma and Pa were even awake . . .

But the Boston clock had run down, and it was Ma's hand shaking him. "I was going to let you sleep in, but Bob Roberts is here. He's dropping Maggie at the farm and thought you might like to go and walk back with her. It's a good chance to get to know her a little. Would you like that?"

He wouldn't; but Maggie too was probably only being pressured by her father. "OK. I'll get dressed."

Maggie moved closer to her father on the single front seat as Rust squeezed in.

"Get you out of bed?" Bob Roberts asked.

"Sort of."

The utility bounced up onto the bitumen and bounced back off it onto the gravel road that led inland to the forest, while Rust tried to work the sleep out of his eyes.

"Bar went last night," Bob Roberts said. "Maggie and Ma usually spend half the day hunting round the swamps for fish and things the grass and reeds have strained out of the flood. The three of you should enjoy that."

Rust felt a deep, painful *clunk* in the pit of his stomach. The bar had gone? Then what about the *Clinker*? He should have gone straight down...

"They won't want me there," Maggie sniffed, when Rust did not respond to her father's words.

"Uh . . . oh yes we will," Rust managed, forcing his mind back to the moment. "You will come. . .?"

Maggie shrugged. "I might."

"Have a nice walk," said Bob, stopping opposite the gate to the dairy farm.

"Thanks." Rust fumbled the door open, wishing everything could speed up so that he could get back and check.

"See you, kids."

Maggie led the way across the road and up the long drive towards the unpainted fibro-sheet house and outbuildings, to the doorway of a shed that Rust realized was the dairy as soon as he saw the stainless-steel boiler and vat inside.

He tried not to breathe in too deeply the smell of the cows he could hear complaining above the sound of a pulsing vacuum pump, and he smiled at the woman in waterboots, trousers and heavy jumper who emerged from an inner door.

"Morning, Maggie, luv," she greeted in a nasal voice, not even bothering to take the hand-rolled butt of the cigarette from between her lips. "This the young Yank?"

"Hi."

"Look just like y' grandad." She filled the two billies that Maggie handed her, but passed them back to Rust.

"Thanks." Rust resisted the impulse to blow away the drip of ash that had fallen from her butt onto the lid of one of the billies. He hoped they didn't have to stay and talk.

"See youse t'morrer, Mags. And you."

"Bye." Rust backed out quickly, lifting the billy and blowing at the ash the moment the woman was out of sight. But it was stuck. Yuk!

"I'll carry ours," Maggie said, following him.

He handed her the billy with the ash on its lid, feeling guilty and hoping she was used to it, and turned back down the driveway, surprised at the flatness of the paddocks beyond the road below, and at the large pools of brown water. Had the whole valley been flooded last night?

"The water comes right up to the road before the bar breaks," Maggie explained. "Right across the road, sometimes."

Rust nodded, trying to imagine the days when Pa's great Shires and Clydesdales grazed across those paddocks, and on these other paddocks now beside him, and when they reached the road he felt a deep sadness at the sight of the beautifully split and mortised post-and-rail fences that now leaned in places, and in others were even broken down.

"He's saving all that for *you*," Maggie said, and her voice sounded so bitter that Rust looked at her in shock.

"*You'll* never come back and farm it," she continued, almost sneering, he thought, not looking at him, her face held straight ahead. "It means nothing to you, and my father would give *anything* for it. But he hasn't got the money, and your Pa wouldn't sell it anyway, in case *you* want it."

"Wh-what would your father do with it?"

"He'd build a house here, with an orchard and vegetable gardens, and a paddock for goats and sheep. He'd make it beautiful."

Rust did not answer. Was this the real reason she had not been friendly from the start? It sounded as though she was telling him something her family had talked about often. Perhaps they had, wishing they could own some land of their own. It would fit in with their lifestyle. A little orchard and farm, goats and sheep so they could spin their own wool. . .

"But your Pa always talks about *you* coming back," she resumed, and he was sure she *was* sneering now and felt angry and guilty. He didn't want to let Pa down, but he *couldn't* come back. What did he know about farming? He didn't even like the thought of it. He was simply not that kind of person.

"I don't want the land," he said at last. "But I don't want to hurt Pa either." He had a sudden idea. "Maybe I could sort of hint to him that your father would like, well, *some* of it? Maybe lease it for now, and then, when. . . Well, one day"—Rust couldn't bring himself to spell it out—"he could get the chance to buy the land."

Maggie stopped, and Rust went on for a few paces before he realized and turned back to face her, surprised at the hope in her eyes; surprised by how pretty she looked when she was not hiding her feelings under a sort of sourness.

"Would you. . .? Would you talk to him about it?"

He nodded. "Sure. I think he'd like to see some of it being used again. I think he'd like to see your father working it."

She smiled then, a fresh-morning smile that did strange things in his chest, and he turned back quickly to walk on, not wanting to give away anything by the smile that had risen to his own face. Perhaps a smile and a blush. . .

"Thank you," she said, catching up. She said it in a kind of whisper.

Neither of them spoke again till they were at his gate, and Maggie didn't look at him or even stop when she asked, "Come surfing with Dad and me tomorrow morning? Early?"

"Hey, can I? Thanks!"

Rust stopped by the gate and watched her as she hurried off; then he turned in, taking time to close the gate after him and to hear with satisfaction the click of the rusty latch. How long was it since *that* had been used? It looked and felt good now. Today he'd start putting the fallen pickets back in place.

He swung the billy round in a circle, ignoring a half-fear that centrifugal force might let him down on this side of the world. Then, as he made his way along the side of the house, he suddenly remembered what he had meant to do this morning, really early.

He *had* to get the storm-tie on the *Clinker* before Pa went. But then Pa wouldn't go too early. Still, it might be better if he just put the billy down and went now. It would only take a couple of minutes. . .

"I wish you'd wait for Rust, Alfred," Ma's voice came impatiently from behind the door.

"I want t' check 'er, Nellie. I hardly slept for worryin'."

Rust plopped the billy down and sprinted for the tea-tree path, almost running over the top of a rabbit caught unawares. He dashed straight to the locker, his eyes registering with surprise the wide mudflats and the thin little creek on the dune side. He had the lid of the locker half up, to get the second tie, before he realized that she was—

Gone?

The lid clattered closed as he leapt to the head of the jetty, desperate eyes opening wide with shock.

The *Clinker* was gone!

Rust looked wildly behind to the entrance of the track. Pa's head was just appearing. He scrambled away along the bank. She must have stuck on the bar. She *must* have—

"Hey!"

Rust skidded to a stop at the shout. Mr Taylor! What did *he* want?

"Oh, there's the old bloke," Mr Taylor went on, and started in the direction of Pa, who was just crossing the bank.

Rust hesitated for an instant, wondering if he should go and stand beside his great-grandfather, wanting to protect him. But it was more important right now to get to the bar, and he fled.

He knew nothing of the short conversation that followed...

"Mr Stewart."

Pa glanced towards the approaching man, and barely acknowledged him with a nod as he continued to the jetty, sucking in a deep harsh breath of bewilderment at the sight of the bare tie-rings.

"Lost the boys yesterday," Mr Taylor said. "Bought young Shaun an air-rifle to amuse him and they went off hunting and got caught in the storm."

Pa had trouble focusing on the empty mooring. The wide mud was bereft of any mark to suggest that Rust might have dragged her across to the channel. But he wouldn't have been able to move her anyway.

"Heard 'em shouting out over on the other bank just before the rain, so I borrowed—" He looked at the jetty, and along the bank. "Where's your rowboat? We pulled her well up right here before we ran for shelter. I just came down now to tie her back to the jetty and put the oars away. Didn't have time last night in the rain."

"Y' *pulled* 'er up?" Pa gasped, swaying slightly.

"Right here. Didn't want her drifting..." His voice trailed off, his eyes searching the mudflats before they settled on the tiny figure of Rust running for the break in the bar...

"Looks like I might have to buy you another one."

Chapter Six

Sand cliffs three metres high rose from a bed twenty metres wide, cut and washed flat by the torrent that had rushed out when the bar gave way. Now, only a thin stream of brown water ran along one side from the outlet of the narrow creek that yesterday had been the wide sailing-waters of the Inlet.

The edge of the cliff gave way abruptly beneath Rust's feet, but he made no attempt to throw himself back, letting the collapsing sand carry him to the bottom, still standing, staring in bleak despair at . . . nothing.

She was gone. Gone out to the sea she had come from—and all because he had been too frightened of ghosts to storm-tie her.

He plodded off along the wide chute, the cliffs lower and lower till they were level with the beach at about the high-water mark. But the tide was almost at full ebb now, and the water from the ranges running out across the glistening flat stained the lacy edges of the water brown; stained brown, too, the waves and the rolling break-foam out at sea. What had Pa said? You could see it for miles? Did that mean that if the *Clinker* wasn't already somewhere on the exposed rocks, she could be out at sea, perhaps still whole if she was afloat?

He'd search the rocks, in case she had gone out and been swept back in on them and was grinding to pieces. Then, if she wasn't back against the rocks, he would search the sea, the beaches. . .

With a quick glance back up the cut through the bar—though he knew Pa could not have reached it yet, even if he was angry enough to try the long walk—Rust turned left, breaking into a run along the beaches below the old signal station, past the place where they had picnicked and Pa had carved the little cuttlebone *Clinker*; the shoreline where that day he had searched so happily with Ma for shells to take home. He ran right on round to the point, searching the rocks out to sea.

But there was no sign of her.

He turned and ran back, sprinting when he reached the cut bar until he was well past and could look out along the edges of the rock shelf. But she wasn't there either, so he swung round and ran back towards the dunes, dropping to a walk through the dry sand and then to a slogging climb, using his hands to help him, up the face of the dunes to their ridge, from where he looked back out to sea.

The brown stain ran in a long curving horn to the west, but there was no gleam of white on it. Perhaps she had been tumbled through the bar and sunk? But Pa was certain to have built buoyancy tanks into her for the safety of the child she was intended for, so even if she was filled, even with a side stove in, she wouldn't be on the bottom. She *couldn't* be! And she didn't have to be on the stain, after all: the stain would be following the ocean currents not the wind, and the wind was from the west now, almost against the run of the Inlet water that had gone to sea. . .

Rust looked east, across to the white boil of the Tambourine which opposed and tore at the storm swells. But even though he stayed watching for several minutes, there was no sign of her there either.

He returned his eyes to the west as a shadow, like a giant manta-ray, swept across the sea and up over the dunes; and he shivered as it took the warmth of the sun for a moment, and noticed the low blue-black clouds above the ranges to the west. Another storm?

He walked back down the dune in long jarring strides,

and again turned east. He would have to search *beyond* the point along the beaches he didn't know—that was the most likely place for the wind to have driven her. If he was wrong, and she had come ashore on this side, then at least there was a sandy beach for her to be driven on to. He had no idea what the shore was like on the other side: neither Dad nor Grandad had ever said much about it. It might be all cliff and rock.

Back again he went to the broken bar, with still nobody in sight, then on past the picnic spot and back to the point. The ebb made rounding it easy—flat wet sand amongst the rocks, so that he did not even have to climb—and there before him was another short half-moon of sand in a beach scalloped from the cliffs.

But no wreck.

He plodded on towards the next point. What had Pa done on discovering the *Clinker* gone? Maybe at first he'd thought that she had broken both her ties and that he, Rust, had gone to search for her. But as soon as he'd opened the locker he would have seen that the other tie had not been used. Pa must know by now that he had been lied to last night.

Rust made a plaintive mewing sound as he climbed the rockfall at the end of the beach and halfway round to the next. Suddenly he felt his feet give way, and an exclamation of despair jerked from his throat.

"Help!"

But there was no-one there to help as the rocks gave way beneath one foot and he clutched desperately at higher ones and found them loose, found himself tumbling away from the fall with one of them still in his hand.

"*Help!*" he cried out again as he went over backwards, and the harsh edge of a rock jagged into the back of his left shoulder.

His feet threw water up into his face as they landed in the deep rockpool which he had climbed the rockfall to avoid, and he gasped as he began to sink, shutting his eyes for a brief instant as his head went under. Then he thrashed out with his arms, feeling no pain yet from his shoulder, panicking at imaginings of what might lurk below, and struggling furiously until he was out and scrabbling his way around the edges of the rockfall, slipping and stumbling.

"No!" he shouted against the booming of the surf as he slipped again. "*No!*" He sought for a foothold, heaved to his feet and sprang across the surge of a swell that welled up under him, teetered on a slippery rock, and lunged as his foot went out from under him. Gasping now, and clawing his way forward and tumbling down onto the wet sand on the other side of yet another scalloped beach, he crawled just ahead of a dying wave onto the thin strip of dry under the cliffs and collapsed on his stomach, exhausted.

His fingers dug into the sand as if to grip the beach, and he closed his eyes. He had let Pa down so badly, let them all down: Mom, Dad, Grandad, Granny. If only he had admitted last night that he'd been frightened off the bank by whatever those flying figures were. . . The *Clinker* would still be safe. Instead of lying here, he would now be hunting the drained swamplands with Ma, and perhaps Maggie too—finding the small pools where at times fish as long as your arm had been trapped by the sudden fall of the water; scooping the tiny dime-sized silver bream; or even picking them out of the tussocks they would have swum into with the rising flood. You ate them fried in butter, with only their heads chopped off (Dad had said), if you could beat the waterbirds to them—waterbirds that just appeared from nowhere the morning the bar broke. . .

He groaned aloud and got to his hands and knees, bruised, not even aware of the blood that had soaked from under his shoulder into his shirt. The shoulder just seemed a little stiffer than the other, the pain from when he had fallen now dulled by the cold.

Be careful, he told himself. You've always been warned to be careful of the rocks when you're alone.

He got to his feet and looked up the eroded gully that cut the cliffs here, carrying now a minor torrent of orange water that leapt and spurted and swirled down its narrow bouldered bed, and spewed ferociously out onto the sand to become tame and spreading and slow, seemingly reluctant to lose its individuality in the heaving ocean, and leaving a stain of its going on the sea.

He could climb that gully, and even if he slipped he would be in no danger from its waters. The worst they could do was roll him over once or twice before a rock gave him the chance to get back to his feet.

But if he climbed it, he would be giving the *Clinker* up for lost; so he splotted through the shallow orange flow towards the next headland, dismayed when he found there was another climb to make: another jump across a narrow channel that filled with heaving bulges of water as the swells came in, the long trailing ribbons of brown kelp streaming in and out with the movement of the sea, and sending a shiver through Rust's body as he jumped.

He landed and scuttled across the remaining rocks like a frightened crab, continuing on hands and feet to the dry sand at the base of . . . *dunes*. Dunes, he saw with a vast relief, that ran into the distance of mists along a wide, open beach.

He sat and pulled his knees up and wrapped his arms around them, the warmth of the sun on his back. He knew that if the *Clinker* was washed up anywhere along here, she would be safe from being broken up. There were no rocks at all that he could see.

He dropped his chin onto his knees—"Ouch!" The sudden sting in his back at the movement brought a realization that the whole of his left shoulder throbbed.

He put his right hand round to feel, and winced. Was it cut? He inspected the fingers of his hand: pale, water-washed blood.

What now? Go on along this beach? He shook his head. Perhaps if he just climbed to the top of this dune and looked out to sea, then made his way back to the Inlet and walked that beach. . . If he couldn't see anything from the dune, she had probably gone with the current rather than the wind and should come ashore on the long home beach.

Nothing. He squinted and gazed out as far as he could see but there was no sign of her, so he turned and made his way along the dune. The sound of an engine surprised him and he squatted in the cover of a cushion-bush as a car went past just inland and above him. He hadn't realized he would be so close to the highway here.

Rust hurried until the dune ended abruptly and he found himself in low coastal bushland. He followed a narrow walking-track, aware when he came to the orange stream again that he was cutting across behind the cliffs he had walked around.

He clambered down its sharp bank, sprang across rocks to cross it, and got hold of a protruding root on the other side to haul himself back. There was the old signal station, dead ahead.

Good—he'd use it for a lookout. Heartened a little, Rust broke into a run, and was nearly there when he had to swerve unexpectedly and drop to his stomach in the shelter of the low heath. Pa and Maggie were climbing the path towards it, carrying . . . yes, a telescope between them.

Rust wormed his way through the heath until he was in higher shelter, and then ran, stooped over, in an arc that brought him back to the low cliff on the bank. He stopped near its edge and crouched, looking past the new timber and the houses to the jetty. It looked so odd: the familiar deck, which had always seemed to float just above the water, was now a bleak platform standing on tall poles above black mud. And no *Clinker* riding peacefully alongside.

He dropped over the cliff and ran along beneath it, using it to conceal him from the watchers above. When he reached the beginning of the bar he stopped again to check quickly along the sand in case Ma, or anyone, was out looking for him. They must surely have missed him by now.

He ran the bar to the edge of the break. Already the sand cliffs had begun to cave as the new floodtide pushed in, riffling against the water coming out and creating cross-waves that undermined the banks and began the building of a new bar.

He slid down the cliff and sloshed across at an angle to come out lower down, where there was no climb. He felt tired, his shoulder hurt now, and he really just wanted to eat something and lie down and get warm. With Pa gone out, Ma would be sympathetic. But that wouldn't bring the *Clinker* back—or alter the fact that he had lied.

There was a creek a mile or so up the beach, Dad said. Perhaps she had got swept round into there.

Rust sighed and plodded off along the beach, hoping Olly or Blue would come over the dunes to fish and ask him what was wrong. *They'd* be sympathetic too. But he couldn't just go and ask them for help; not the kind of help he needed.

It took fifteen minutes before he saw the break in the dunes ahead, but when he reached the creek he was quite dismayed by his own lack of logic in even remotely believing that she might have been swept in here. This creek had burst out across the beach too. It was smaller, and the remains of the sand cliffs rose up no higher than his knees, but the water *had* burst a way through and was only now beginning to run back in on the flood—like the Inlet.

He bent down, scooped with cupped hands and drank.

"Yush!" Pure seawater! But he was just so thirsty. Perhaps on the flats above?

After walking back along the creek for some distance, Rust climbed the scrubby bank. There were puddles lying in the hollows, and he knelt down beside the largest and, dipping a finger, tasted a few drops. It seemed fresh. But he didn't want to risk stirring up the mud. He bent forward and sucked directly from the surface till his thirst was quenched, then sat back on his heels and gazed in the direction of the ranges, wondering, as he had often wondered here and in comparable country back home, how the first settlers had ever had the courage to come out from the cities and hack farmland from the wilderness.

Stiffly he got to his feet and stood on the edge of the bank, looking out to sea. There was still no sign of her, and he decided he would just have to go on to the next point and look from there. He shook his head to cut off further thought, and slid back down to the beach, crossing the inflow to the creek close to the sea where it seemed shallowest and going on along the hard.

A pair of hooded dotterels ran suddenly from beside a partly buried branch above the high-tide line, and Rust wondered if they had come from a nest. But he didn't go up to see; he didn't really care any more. He just trudged on, not interested in the shells, the weed, the driftwood, or even in the huge snowy cuttlebone—which Pa would have liked for carving—rolled right up to his feet by a wave. He ignored the cries of the gulls, excited by the banquet laid on the beach by the storm, and disregarded the lone albatross that coasted above him and the spatter-ing of rain that chilled him.

And then the sand ended and he had to clamber over rocks—cautiously, favouring his left arm—to make his way out to the point and round far enough to look beyond it to the rocky shoreline, and into the deep gully cut by another creek.

But there was no sign of the *Clinker*, he might just as well not have come—except perhaps to go up the valley a little way for Dad, who had said he wanted him to see the bright green fields of the flats in what was something akin to a gorge; the fields and the small slab cottage. He walked in a little way. Dad would be disappointed to hear that the cottage was just an abandoned shell now, and the fields a high tangle of encroaching mimosa scrub.

Around him, as if in some weird dream, he became aware of the statue-still heads of twenty or more grey kangaroos, waiting in freeze-frame to see if they were under threat from this boy who seemed to have come up out of the sea. For a moment Rust was tempted to clap his hands, just to see them bound. But instead he shrugged and turned back, even less interested in the shore now than on the way here, his mind on how best to cut this holiday short. Perhaps he could sneak back into the house to get his ticket and his things, and then hitch back to the airport. He wouldn't even need to take his clothes: they could be sent on.

He dropped to his knees and kept still. Someone was coming down the face of the dune up ahead. Two people. Had they been sent to search for him? He watched them keenly, easing forward until he was lying on his stomach. They continued to the hard and stopped, facing the sea. They seemed to have . . . rods. Olly and Blue!

Rust scrambled up and broke into a jog. Olly and Blue were the two people in this whole country, and that included Ma and Pa, that he felt he could really trust.

"Hi!" he shouted as he came within hailing distance. "Olly, Blue!"

They turned and waited till he came up, Blue winking a greeting and Olly's stomach shaking. "Y' look like y've been left out in the rain by mistake."

"I was looking for our boat."

"Flood take her?" Blue asked. "Must have really gone with a rush last night. Reckon you better go on home and warm up. You'll spend your holiday in bed if you don't, by the look of you."

"Uh . . . the sun might come out again in a minute." Rust looked with hope to the sky, saw the leaden clouds, and searched desperately in his mind for some other reasonable excuse for staying here on the beach with them. "I'll build a fire from driftwood."

"Stick this on." Blue slipped off the padded jacket he was wearing against the cold, realizing that something was wrong, glancing to Olly and getting a slight shake of the head in return. Olly could sense it too, but had no idea what.

"Thanks." Rust pushed his left arm into the sleeve of the jacket.

"What the blazes have you done t' your back?" Blue recoiled as he reached for the jacket to help the boy. "Crikey! That's not a mozzie bite, mate."

"I fell on a rock," Rust mumbled, feeling tears prickle at his eyes; ashamed of them, and tired, and desperate.

The two men glanced at each other and reached an unspoken agreement. Blue helped Rust with the other arm. "Zip it right up." He looked to the boiling storm sea and shook his head. "Bit too miserable for me, mate. Think I'll go back and stoke a blaze."

"You're readin' my mind again," Olly chortled. "Come up and have a bit of a warm-up with us, Rusty?"

"Thanks." Rust knew they were giving up their fishing for his sake, and was grateful. He pulled the hood of the jacket up and snugged his hands deep in its pockets, the warmth flooding into his body from more than the mere donning of the jacket and the climb up and over the dunes to the secluded hollow in their lee.

"Tinder, tea and tucker," Blue said, standing his rod and hanging his creel from a hook in the dense matted overhang of the dune trees in front of the tent. He squatted and began feeding with tiny branches the coals of the old fire still alive under an iron frame, and by the time they were crackling Olly had gathered larger dead pieces to add in until the flames could support the wet logs already axed into lengths in a neat stack by the fire.

"All the 'ome comforts," Olly said, seeing the way Rust's eyes moved about the site. "If it's not good enough for mum, it's not good enough f' me." He shook with silent laughter as he filled a billy out of a large plastic bottle and hung it from the iron frame.

"Right. Jacket off," Blue ordered, and when it was off he indicated the sand in front of the fire. "Sit down there and have a bit of a gaze into the bush television."

Rust sat, pulling his legs up and circling them with his arms, his chin resting on his knees, teeth pressed tightly together. He couldn't really expect them to be gentle.

"Aw, it doesn't look much worse'n Blue gets when he shaves." Rust felt Blue's fingers lifting the back of his T-shirt, and winced at a sudden bite.

"Take it easy," Blue said. "We'll give it a bit more soaking than the rain's managed, and then put something on it." He poured hot water from the billy into a basin and added cold before he began dribbling it over the dark bloodstain, while Olly made tea.

"With or without milk?" Olly asked Rust as he set out three enamel mugs. "If it's with, you have t' close your eyes and use y' imagination."

Rust tried to smile. "Ouch!" Even the mug's handle was hot.

"Y' sit it in front of you as a radiator for the first half-hour," Blue advised, using one hand for his mug and the other to continue the water-dribbling. "You been past the point looking?" Rust nodded. "Hope she comes back in. Bit of a shame t' lose a beauty like that. Surprised you didn't have her secured against that sort of storm. Would have thought your grandfather knew by now what can happen."

Rust nodded dumbly, the fire seeming to lose its warmth, the hot sweet tea its flavour. "He did," he said suddenly. "He knew and told me what to do and I didn't."

Olly and Blue exchanged a glance.

"Yeah . . ." Blue breathed. "Well, that wouldn't make you feel so good, would it? Get your arms unwound and we'll see if she'll come away." He took a pinch of shirt between his fingers and lifted gently. "Just shout if it hurts."

Rust tensed. "Uh, a bit." He clenched his teeth.

"Want me to stop?" Rust shook his head. "Arms up then."

"Ouch!"

"She's right," Blue said quickly. "Get back into that tea now. Had a tetanus shot lately?"

"A few weeks ago. It was one of the ones I had to have before I left."

Olly and Blue considered the wound, a depression with the skin torn in a short jag. "One of them antidispeptic pads," Olly decided. "Bit of that gauze and a heap of stickin'-plaster. I'll get the kit."

Rust sipped at the tea while Olly disappeared down a narrow track. The sound of a cardoor slamming shut came a minute or so later.

"How are the grandparents taking it, Rust?"

"I don't know. When I saw she was gone I just started searching."

"Yeah, well, I guess you're not too keen on going back in till you find her."

"I can't."

"No. Might be a bit of a long shot, though."

"Here we are." Olly squatted down with the first-aid kit, a battered tin with part of what Rust guessed was a red cross showing through paint splatters. "Now, you pad 'er up and I'll tape, Blue old mate."

"Share a bite of tucker with us?" Blue asked when they were finished.

"The old people might be a bit worried about him," Olly said.

"Yeah, well, he's not real keen on going back right now, Oll. What about it, Rust?"

Rust nodded gratefully. Blue broke a forked branch, dug it into the sand in front of the fire and spread the T-shirt across it. "Shame it had to be you.instead of those couple of dudes with the tape-player who pushed her off the bar the day of the fog."

Rust's head snapped up. "Huh?"

"The kids that were up here hunting round with an air-rifle yesterday."

"They what. . .?"

"Shoved your boat off the sand the day of the fog."

"Oh. . ." Rust looked into the fire. So he hadn't just been careless that first time. Could they also have gone into the house and knocked the *Ohio*'s lamp off the dresser? He sighed. Did it matter any more anyway? Not tying the *Clinker* last night was so much worse than pushing her off the bar or breaking the lamp.

"A feed!" Blue stated heartily, reading the renewed despair in the boy's face. "Ever heard of a damper?"

"Dad and Grandad always cook them when we're on a picnic at home."

"The old bloke been over there too, eh?" Olly said, then saw Rust's puzzlement. "You said grandfather. . ."

"Yes. This one's my *great*-grandfather."

"Crikey." Olly let out a silent whistle. "I thought they only ever had them in fairy stories. How old is he?"

"Uh, eighty-five."

"Struth," Olly whispered, lost for further words.

"How about you throwin' the damper, Rust?" Blue suggested. "We've been doing *all* the work."

"'K," Rust agreed tonelessly.

Blue brought a tin of flour and a packet of salt, then washed out the dish he had used for soaking Rust's back.

"And don't use the spoon in the tin for stirring. That's our dry'un. Find a bit of stick."

"Where's the baking-powder?"

Olly wheezed, his stomach bouncing. "It's not the Ritz, mate."

Rust looked from one to the other. "Will it work without it?"

"Wind 'er up and see," Olly suggested.

Rust mixed up the dough of flour, salt and water with a short twig that he first stripped free of bark. He sprinkled more flour in, picked up the dough and began to knead.

"That's a bit flash, isn't it?" Blue observed.

"Dad says it gives it some life if you can get the gluten working."

"We didn't have any gluten—did we?" Olly looked over to Blue.

"Gluten's part of the flour," said Rust.

"Bloody Yanks!" Olly shook his head.

Rust grinned to himself, the worry receding for the time being, and he continued working the dough until it was firm and elastic. He moulded it into a ball and raked out a bed for it with the mixing-stick.

"Hang on, we're not totally primitive," Olly protested, reaching for a box of foil. He stripped off enough for Rust to wrap the dough in. "And a nice little salmon each?" he suggested to Blue.

"Go for the doctor!" Blue agreed, pulling the top off a foam box and selecting three scaled and cleaned fish. Olly put dobs of margarine in their gut cavities, added a splash of wine, and wrapped them up and placed them amongst the coals. "That's the cordon bleu in me. Cook up another cuppa while we wait, Blue."

Rust fingered his T-shirt where it hung on the forked stick, and turned it. There were still showers, he could see them drifting across the valley like. . . He thought of the almost invisible gauze curtains floating from the seabreeze at the open window in Andrew Wyeth's painting. Yes, gauze curtains drawn across the valley on invisible rails, but with the roof of the dune trees a dense matting—grey-green leaves above, an underceiling of dead and partly rotten leaves below—so that only the occasional drip came through until the wind shook down a shower. And in the warmth of the fire, that much hardly mattered.

"Seen these?" Blue held out something like a bent tube of rough stone. "Calcified root-hollow of one of these trees' grandaddies. Put it in your pocket to take home. Tell 'em it's a bit from an Aboriginal natural-gas pipeline. Yanks'll believe anything."

Rust smiled and slipped it into his pocket. It was odd, but he had a feeling that the best memory he was going to take back of Australia would be of sitting here, in the darkness of this tree-cavern, with the odd drips of water hissing in the coals of the fire when the wind shook the branches; of sand that took your shape when you moved your backside to get comfortable; of the sound of muted storm-breakers; of the smell of damper and fish, and the taste of hot sweet tea; and of a tall red-headed guy with an amused grin and his dark-haired tubby pal with a belly heaving in often-silent laughter and dark eyes that laughed *all* the time.

It was nothing like the dream, nothing like the plans, and what had happened last night would always be a bitter memory.

"Tucker cooked?"

"Reckon." Blue used a forked stick, which had obviously been put to a similar purpose before, to lift the fish and damper from the coals. Olly added wood to build the fire back to crackling life.

"Just like mother makes!" Olly rolled his eyes blissfully, drawing in a deep lungful of the aroma of the damper when Blue broke it open.

"Dob 'er while she's still hot," Blue commanded, reaching for the margarine, a knife standing upright from its centre.

Rust dobbed, and the damper stained sunshine-yellow. Blue opened a fish and set it in front of him with a blackened fork to eat it with. "Go for it, young Russell!"

"Ah, y' common coast-salmon, or bay trout, depending on where you was dragged up," Olly sighed contentedly. "Haven't any softdrink for ya, Rust, so what'll it be while we bury a beer?"

"Nothing, thanks."

They didn't talk much while they ate. A little about their life as painters and decorators, which seemed to consist mostly of hilarious accidents for which they denied any responsibility—although Rust found himself doubting that disclaimer—and mention of a wife and bludging children for Blue and a mother he couldn't bear to leave for Olly. Then, when they had all finished eating, the two men turned to Rust.

"Well?" Blue began. "What now, mate? Olly and I are due back in a couple of days—or it might have been yesterday," he added thoughtfully. "So we'll take you back to Tulla if you like."

"Tulla?"

"Tullamarine. The airport."

"Oh . . . I was thinking of going back sooner, thanks."

Blue turned to Olly. "I think it probably *was* yesterday."

"I think it was," the other agreed, his stomach heaving with silent laughter. "Take you up t'night then, if you like."

Rust's spirits rose.

"*If* it's okay with your great-grandparents," Blue added.

Rust sighed. "Thanks anyway, but I'll be fine." He got up. He couldn't stay here forever, though he would forever remember being here. "I'd better start looking again." He took his T-shirt off the branch and pulled it on, having some brief difficulty when it caught on the plaster.

"How's it feel?" Blue asked.

"It's not hurting. Thanks for lunch, and for being such good friends, and, and everything."

"Well, you know where to find us," Olly said, "because I think Blue's probably got the dates wrong again."

"Is that right, mate?" Blue retorted. "And who was supposed t' be notchin' the tree?"

"*You* cut the bloody thing down for the fire," Olly accused. "See ya, Rusty."

Going back up the dune was the hardest climb Rust had ever made, the warm cavern of friendship he had left behind drawing him back like a magnet, turning the wind bitter, the rain into sleet, the ocean into a malignant thing of heaving wickedness.

He glanced back from the ridge and saw the dark-green roof of the cavern below, picked it by the whisper of blue smoke that rose just above the leaves before it was ripped apart by the turbulence of the wind and lost—lost as surely as the warmth and friendliness down in that hollow.

Tears blended with the rain on his cheeks, and he plunged down the storm-side of the dunes in jerking strides, not trying, for the first time since he was a little kid, to hold back the tears. And then he saw a figure standing on the beach out from the bar, dress flapping away from rubber boots—a sad, lonely figure lost in the driving grey cold of a bitter squall—and he dropped and rolled behind a tussock of wind-streamed marram grass and lay still; but only for a moment. Ma was looking for him. She'd be so desperate.

He scrambled to his feet and ran towards her. If he could just talk to her . . .

"Ma!" he cried, though she was too far away to hear;

but he called anyway, because she looked so alone. He stumbled, and cried her name out again in despair, but all at once threw himself flat and rolled behind another clump of grass as three more dark figures came out onto the beach towards her and she turned to face them. Mr Taylor and the two boys!

"Go away," he sobbed quietly. "Just go *away.*"

Chapter Seven

Shaun and Tony walked past along the beach below, heavily rugged up, hands deep in their coat pockets, looking now ahead, now down at the sand, and Rust was glad the wash of the floodtide waves was removing any footprints he may have left—if they were searching for him. Perhaps they were looking for the *Clinker*.

He swung his eyes back to where Ma stood with Mr Taylor, squinting against a sudden swirl of rain that seemed to bounce off his face, and he noticed that his skin was numb with cold. Why was Mr Taylor with Ma?

Trying to persuade her to go back with him, he realized, as Mr Taylor's hand reached out; and he saw the way Ma reluctantly took the man's arm, the way she began walking back with him towards the end of the cliffs and the beach that led to the bank of the Inlet.

Rust let tears fall without any attempt to stop them, feeling suddenly cast-out, isolated and alone, and so far, so very far from home. He was in a strange country, amongst strange people—he had a fleeting sense of fellowship with the survivors of the *Ohio*—and so cold. But where could he go to get warm? Back to the camp in the lee of the dunes?

He sighed. He'd certainly be welcome there; but Olly and Blue would begin to feel responsible for him, would want to take him back to Ma and Pa, and it would get so involved. . . He was too young for all this: he should never have come to Australia by himself.

His body began to shake with the cold, and he turned and wormed his way up the face of the dune, his left shoulder hurting if he put too much weight on his arm. As soon as he was over the top he stood up, and could see Ma and Mr Taylor on the other side walking along the beach below the cliffs.

The thought of becoming involved with Mr Taylor and the two boys—and that seemed inevitable now if he went back—was the final straw. He'd go home. He'd get his wallet and some clothes from his bedroom and just go. He would ring them from the airport once he had a plane, and he'd ring them again from home when he was there and tell them he was sorry; tell them he hadn't tied the *Clinker* last night, tell them anything anyone wanted him to, just so long as he was home.

He stumbled and slid down the side towards the Inlet, keeping to the cover of the trees and grass until he was nearly at the mud, then breaking into a run back towards the inland end until he was far enough to be out of sight of anyone on the banks near the houses. There, he turned and sloped across to the channel, the water running inland now on the floodtide, and began to swim, surprised to find the water warm.

The wind cut him again as he climbed out on the other side, and he ran across the mud and through the swamp-grass towards the protection of the tea-tree, the patch on his shoulder squelching as he jogged along the sandy track. When he was close to the house, he stopped and squatted down to watch through the palisades of the twisted trunks for a minute, before standing in a crouch and slipping between the trees until he could look through the lounge-room window into the kitchen beyond. Pa was there, seated in front of the stove, bent forward staring into the fire, and Rust guessed that Ma and Mr Taylor had not arrived yet. There was a sudden dull pain in his chest, and he felt anger and sadness mixing inside him.

Shivering from cold and distress, Rust slipped across to the window of his bedroom and climbed through. He got out a fresh T-shirt, socks, the long trousers he had arrived in and a pullover; slipped the wallet, containing his money, ticket and passport, into his pocket; and paused to listen again. He was sure he could hear Pa's deep, rasping breaths.

He backed towards the window, the wet clothes in one hand and sneakers in the other, carefully wiping away the wet footprints with the sleeve of his pullover, leaning back over the sill to complete the task when he was out.

Then he waited with his head in the window to listen to the sounds of Pa's breathing again. He sounded bad. But there was nothing Rust could do, nothing that would not make things even worse. Sadness rose within him like a physical pain, the anger now almost forgotten, and he turned and moved back into the trees to find a hiding-place where he could wait till evening.

He didn't need to go far, and snugged himself down amongst tall tussocks in a small clearing, the house still in sight. As he was balling the wet clothes to hide them, he found the piece of calcified root Blue had given him. He would take that back. Everything else could be sent later.

He bent his legs and rested his chin on his knees, watching the house, thinking of home. It would be night-time in Boston, or very early morning, and Mom and Dad would probably be asleep. What would they do if they knew he was out here hiding, hunkered down like some hunted animal, planning an escape from the two people they would imagine he loved second-most in the whole world?

Well, he wouldn't tell them how all of that had changed. He would make up some story, a tale that would work in with whatever Ma said to them on the phone when she called to say he had gone. He would make up a story that would not destroy *their* memories and feelings for Ma and Pa.

Or perhaps it would be better just to tell the truth. . .

He changed position, making himself comfortable against

a friendly trunk on the edge of the grass patch. Finding a twig, he scratched in the sand.

An ant came across the flat and began to climb a small hillock, and Rust used the twig to pull the sand gently away behind it so that no matter how doggedly it laboured to climb, the receding sand slid it back. It didn't seem as if the tiny insect would ever realize it was on a treadmill; would ever abandon its singleminded purpose of proceeding straight ahead. Rust felt a sudden surge of fellow-feeling, and let it go.

Would humans ever find something like an ant on a distant planet? Science-fiction stories often had ants as the intelligent life, usually ants about the size of a crane and with at least as much power, but with a lot more mobility and a hunger for the flesh of human explorers.

He grinned bitterly to himself, then jerked his head up at the sound of his name being called.

"Ru—ust. . .! Ru—ust. . .!"

She must have stopped down near the jetty.

"Ru—ust. . .!" Ma's cry brought back the ache of sadness in his chest. If only Mr Taylor wasn't with her.

He heard the scrape and clack of the back door. How would Pa react to Mr Taylor? Not violently any more; probably not even strongly, judging by the way he had looked through that window—bent forward over the fire, the heart gone out of him. All at once, the pungent scent of smoke blew down: Ma must have added wood to the stove, probably because Pa was chilling again. The boy shivered, and yawned, noticing at last just how tired he was. Perhaps it would be sensible to try to sleep for a while. He looked about. There was a curtain of New Zealand spinach draped from the low crowns of the tea-tree a little further back, and he crawled across on hands and knees and poked his head through the leafy vines that fell like a beaded flyscreen to the sand.

Bones! Rabbits' bones, he guessed; and maybe fish-bones too. A fox's lair? It looked cosy, anyway, and if he curled up way at the back he would be safe from any casual search.

He crawled through, collecting the crushed skull of a rabbit as he went, and snuggled down against a trunk at the rear, adjusting his position until the soggy pad on his shoulder fitted into a bend in the wood. He studied the skull in his hands, and yawned again . . .

An oblong of light showed in the darkness, and Rust moved stealthily forward until he could see through the unlit lounge-room and into the kitchen beyond the inner doorway. He caught a brief glimpse of Ma as she crossed from, he supposed, the stove.

He moved away and hugged himself, chilled, then slid back into the shadows and skirted the house, meeting the track to the garden about halfway down and following it through to the gate.

The strawberries would only make a mushy mess in his pockets if he tried to take any with him, so he ate several, squatting above the plants as he did so, listening to the night.

It was still and silent but for the distant thunder of the surf, the day-old power of the storm still travelling in the driven swells. Then the mournful cry of plover high above clang-lang-langed down across the valley and echoed from the hills, and the boy gave a little shiver that was not quite fear, pulled half-a-dozen carrots and left the garden.

One last look? He hesitated, then moved silently until he could see through the window of the kitchen. Maggie was holding the sugarbowl for Pa, who was seated in front of the stove rugged up in a coat and a woollen muffler. Had he been out searching—or (Rust's heart gave a leap of alarm) was he ill again?

Anne Roberts appeared at the sink, then Ma, doing something that was hidden from view by the sill.

Rust pulled back—and froze. Someone, some thing,

was brushing through the tea-tree! There was the sound of boots on concrete and the rattle of the back-door knob. Those inside, except Pa, turned to look, and Rust saw Bob Roberts appear, shaking his head.

He must have been out searching. Rust leant against a trunk, knowing he should go now but finding it difficult to pull away. Ma looked so desperate. . . Perhaps he should abandon his plans and go back in, if only just for her. Yes, that would be best. He loved Ma. She would put her arms around him, and probably cry, but she'd be happy. He could not bear to see the distress that showed in her face now, distress that would vanish at the mere sight of him.

He started forward, to be pulled up almost immediately by the lift of Pa's head. His eyes looked so wild, and he was saying something to someone, something that looked like anger. Anger towards *him?*

Rust tried to choke down the cry that rose inside him. He turned and blundered away along the path to the gate, tears blinding his eyes. One foot skidded on something. The bolt on the gate struck his hip and snagged his trouser pocket.

"No!" he cried, the material tearing as he jerked away. If only he was home. He just wanted to be home.

He stumbled along the sandy track to the blacktop of the highway and turned along it, running on the bitumen, running until a stitch forced him to drop to a walk. But he couldn't afford to walk yet. Holding the palm of his hand against the pain, he ran on, a wobbling run, until he had left the valley and was moving through the dark winding avenue of the great red ironbarks and judged that he was further out than Bob Roberts would search and could slow to a walk.

What he needed now was a lift. There was usually traffic passing regularly along the road.

Headlights cut the night somewhere ahead, and he moved onto the gravel of the shoulder and walked there, watching as the four beams crested a slight rise, came over it and shone on him, splintered and sharp through the remains of his tears. Rust looked away, grateful when the driver dipped them.

He lifted a hand to say *thanks*, and the driver touched his horn in response, setting up a momentary bond of passing friendship that the boy grasped and held as he plodded on and on along the canyon of tall timber, which broke suddenly on his right, exposing long luminous lines of tumbling foam.

One of the beaches he had searched this morning. Was it really just this morning? It seemed an age ago.

Two more headlights came towards him, but this driver did not dip them and Rust was blinded in the darkness that followed and had to stop to let his eyes readjust. He was about to go on when a third car came, this time from behind. He stepped back onto the edge of the gutter and motioned with his thumb for a ride. The car, which was moving quite slowly anyway, drew to a stop beside him.

"Lose this, mate?" a familiar voice asked, and a hand just inside the window displayed a wallet. Rust's palm slapped down on his torn pocket, and his head dropped.

"Didn't need *clues* to guess where you'd be," Olly said. "Hop in."

Rust stepped forward and reached for the wallet, wondering whether Olly would let him take it or would use it to force him to go back. "Are you going home now?" he asked Olly.

"Ah, weren't planning on it," Olly replied.

"I'm . . . I'm on my way to the airport," Rust said. He reached out for the wallet. "Thanks for bringing it."

"What else are mates for?" Blue called across. "But hop in, young Rusty. The old lady's pretty cut up about your going off. We took in an oar we found on the beach and met them."

"I can't," Rust said, and edged his hand out closer to the wallet. Without his ticket . . .

"You're breakin' 'er 'eart, mate," Olly said softly.

Rust's hand closed over the wallet, and he held his breath as he pulled it towards him.

"Hop in," Olly coaxed, releasing it.

Rust huffed out a short breath of relief and stepped back to the gutter. "Thanks."

"Listen," Blue said. "We're not leaving you out here on y' lonesome."

"You can't force me." Rust backed away, wondering whether if he climbed the cutting behind he could get away far enough to hide.

The door swung open and Olly stepped out, leaning on the top of it, and Rust felt the fight go out of him. He was just a kid, just a little guy against these two.

"We're not going to *make* ya do anything," Olly said, "except come with us. If you're set on shootin' through, then we'll drive you to the airport. We just can't leave you out here hitching on your own."

Rust was cautious. "I want to go to the airport."

Olly sighed. "Righto, then. But hop in." He leaned over, opened the rear door and dropped back into his own seat, and Rust, relieved, joined them.

"We'll have to slip back to the camp and chuck our stuff in," Blue said. "I'm not coming all the way back again just for another couple of days."

"I'm sorry," Rust apologized.

Blue U-turned the car and headed slowly back along the road. "Not interested in the oar we found on the beach?" he asked.

Rust hesitated. It couldn't have belonged to the *Clinker* because there hadn't been any oars in her when she was swept away.

"An *oar*!" There was exasperation in Blue's voice. "Boats have 'em, you know."

"But there weren't any in the *Clinker* when she went off," said Rust. Olly chortled, and the boy was sure he could feel the tremble of his laughter through the seat.

"The way *you* thought she went off," Blue said. "But you was dead wrong, mate."

Rust hunched down in the seat. The car was hardly moving. "But I'm sure I put them away," he whispered.

"Put 'im out of his misery, Oll," said Blue.

"Right. She didn't break her lead, young Russell. A neighbour borrowed her t' fetch his kids back across the water when the storm come in—and didn't tie her when he got her back."

"Mr Taylor!" Rust exclaimed. He thought of the flapping figures that had so terrified him.

"Sounds about the monicker I remember," Olly agreed.

The car speeded up, and the headlights that till now had flickered from the passing trees seemed to disappear. Rust realized that they were travelling across the flats.

"I'll go back," he whispered.

"Good on you, son," Blue said, his voice level. "Don't get too much of a shock when you see the old man, though. He's not looking all that good."

The car slowed and bumped softly onto the sand of the track, and Rust led the way down the side of the house. He stopped abruptly outside the window when he saw her.

Ma was moving towards the sink, and her face made Rust's chest tighten in pain. She looked so old, so desperate, so sad. Maggie was standing next to Pa; her mother and father were in the background. Was *everybody* here?

Olly gave a gentle shove. "Come on," he encouraged.

Ma's head snapped up at the sound of the voice or the glimpse of movement—Rust was not sure which—and then she saw him. For a moment he was sure she would collapse.

"Ma..."

Her hands came up and reached towards him with the glass of the window between them, but then she turned and stumbled for the back door, and Rust bumped past Blue and Olly in his urgency, unaware of the tears streaming down his face.

"Oh, son! Thank the Lord!"

He let her bury him in her arms, and didn't try to check the sobbing.

"Tea," Olly said. "Buckets'a tea. Only thing in moments'uv crisis and confusion. With sugar." He rested a hand on Ma's shoulder. "Loads'uv sugar, that's the secret. Come on, Ma. Let's get the calf inside and kill the fatted prodigal." He gave her shoulder a gentle tug, and she let one arm fall from Rust and started in, her other arm tight around him.

"Pa," she called as they came into the kitchen.

The old man was already on his feet, facing the door, his whole body shaking, his arms reaching out. "I thought they'd come for you, too, son. I thought they'd got you too. . . ."

"Don't be a fool, Alfred." Ma's voice trembled. She moved forward, releasing Rust and taking hold of Pa's arm.

"Mr Stewart," Bob Roberts said softly, moving from a seat to stand beside the old man, one arm going round his shoulders. "You can go to bed, now. He's safe."

Pa swayed slightly; frowned. "Took 'er off from th' bar. . . Broke th' lamp. . ."

"I broke it!" Maggie blurted out. "I didn't mean to break it."

". . . Took th' Clinker back t' th' graveyard. . ."

"But I didn't—" Rust began, his voice overridden by Ma's desperate tone. "Mr Taylor's told you that he didn't tie her!" she pleaded.

"They made 'im," Pa quavered, swaying and then leaning heavily against Bob Roberts.

"Come on, old-timer," Blue said gently. He stepped forward to Pa's free side and put an arm around his waist. "Spot of bed."

"And a nice solid belt o' whisky," Olly added. "You'll be a new man in the morning."

"Was th' *sailors!*" Pa rasped, trembling, his eyes grown so wild that Rust fell back.

"It's all right," Anne Roberts reassured them, putting an arm around Rust. "It's just a fever."

Blue looked to Bob, who nodded, and together they eased the old man towards the door and out of the kitchen, with Ma, her hands knitted in agitation, behind them.

"What was it you said you broke?" Anne asked her daughter when they had gone.

"The lamp, the one from the *Ohio* that was in Rust's room," Maggie whispered, dropping her eyes. "I should have told them, but I was almost glad Rust got into trouble." She looked up at Rust, as if pleading. "I'm sorry. I was in the kitchen cleaning up for Ma when I heard you coming. I ran to your room to get out through the window. I've slept in that room when Mum and Dad have been away. I just *knocked* the lamp. I didn't *mean* to break it."

Rust's shoulders had sagged. "I should never have come."

"Russell! They *needed* you here. It's kept them going for the last year, knowing you were coming." Anne's voice trembled as she spoke. "I'll go and see if I can help your Ma."

"Tea," Olly stated thoughtfully, puzzled by being involved in something he couldn't laugh at. He carried the kettle across to the tap and filled it. "Buckets of it." The tap-handle came off in his hand. "Whoops!" he gurgled. His stomach began to shake helplessly, and Maggie looked to Rust in slight alarm.

"That's just him," Rust whispered. "Has Pa been like this before?"

"Not strange like this."

"Had a bit of a shock," Olly said, poking up the fire

and adding wood. "My Nanna did it when she got old."
His stomach began to shake again at some memory. "My
brother used to put on our grandfather's old hat and coat
and spook her." He shook some more, and had to sit
down. "Terrible things kids do. She used to go after 'im
with her stick. Thought it really *was* grandpa and said she
owed him something. Always wondered what it was. But
each time she was right again the next day—a dose of
whisky and a sleep."

"I hope so," Rust said.

"I don't ever want to be old," Maggie whispered.

"Only way to get to the end of y' life," Olly managed,
still shaking when Blue, Bob and Anne came back.

"Seems to think the ghosts of some wreck are closing
in on him," Blue sighed. "Taken back the boat and now
they'll come for . . ." He looked questioningly to Bob.

"He's built a lot of things from the wreck timbers,"
Bob explained, slipping an arm around his daughter.

"Then if we could get the *Clinker* back," Rust said,
"it'd make him realize . . ."

Bob shrugged. "Anne thought you might like to come
home with Maggie and me. She's going to spend the night
here to give your Ma a hand if she needs it."

"Thanks," Rust said, shaking his head. "I'd rather be
here. I *should* be here."

"Maybe," Bob conceded. "But don't feel you have to."

"Cuppa?" Olly offered, pouring hot water into the
teapot and sitting it on the bricks beside the stove to
warm.

"No thanks. I'll get off and tell the Taylors that Rust's
back, and bring some things over for Anne."

"I don't think we can do much more, Oll," Blue
concluded.

"Not leavin' without a cuppa, mate!"

"You want to stay till I get back with Mum's things,
Maggie?" her father asked. Maggie shook her head. "See
you in a bit then."

"Well," Blue said when they had left. "Think we better put a bit of time into looking for that boat of his tomorrow. Can't imagine she'd go out to sea and stay."

Olly took the tea canister from the shelf above the stove. "Wonder what she *did* owe 'im for," he mused, emptying the teapot and spooning in tealeaves.

"What?" Blue looked puzzled.

Olly snorted with laughter. "It's a long story, mate."

Blue shook his head. "Never run dry, do you? Get your tea brewing." He turned to Rust. "We'll have another look at that shoulder before we shoot through."

They maintained a bright crackle in the fireplace, and Ma brought a second lamp so that there would be no shadows. Well before midnight Pa was sleeping soundly.

"You don't really need to stay all night, Anne."

Anne Roberts looked at the old man and smiled softly. "He's so peaceful. Promise to send Rust for me if anything else happens?"

"I promise. Rust can walk you home."

"I'll be fine."

"I will," Rust said quickly.

He was surprised at the warmth of the night outside: the same silkiness he had noticed in the breeze that first morning.

"It's gone round to the north again," Anne noted, the slap of her leather thongs sharp against the sand of the road. "We're going to have some more hot days."

"It changes quickly here," Rust said. "The weather."

When he left her at the back door, he didn't go back to the road but down the dark tunnel to the riverbank, running in momentary fright when he reached it but making himself stop at the entrance to the track that led home, to look up into the huge bowl of the sky with its myriad glimmering pinpoints. One of them was moving. A satellite? Maybe from home. It was weird, when you thought of being *inside* one.

He dropped his gaze down to the Inlet: the star-slivers reflecting from patches of water on the mud, the dune a dark solid silhouette against the sky, a flicker of. . . He grinned, and the night seemed suddenly friendly. Olly and Blue's fire! They were still up, then. He hadn't expected that the tree-cavern could be seen from here; it probably couldn't be during the day. Taking a final glance at the firelight in the blackness that was the side of the valley at night, he turned and made his way slowly up through the dark tunnel under the tea-tree and let himself discreetly into the house, aware for the first time that there was no key in the lock, that it was never locked. It made him pause. Ma and Pa could never really be happy in America.

"Peaceful as a baby," Ma reported. "Wind's gone round to the north. That'll help his chest, anyway. You'll have to sleep in tomorrow to catch up."

But he couldn't. He woke to the sounds of movement from the kitchen, the scent of eucalyptus on the inland breeze mixing with the sweet smell of woodsmoke and the mutter of low voices.

Anne and Maggie were with Ma in the kitchen. Ma looked tired, but not desperate like last night. "He's still worrying," she said, kissing Rust. "But he's not wandering any more." She could always see the cheerful side. "Number of times I've had your grandfather as a boy delirious from fever, and then off fishing before I was out of bed the next morning!"

"Goin' up th' station t' watch 'er onto th' reef," Pa said, surprising them all as he appeared in the doorway.

"Alfred!" Ma cried out, her confidence slipping.

"She'll go on th' Tambourine t'day," he said, nodding to Anne and Maggie, then pulling a chair to the table. "North wind an' all, she'll come back on th' flood an' go t' pieces on th' reef." He looked to the window. "Got about an hour. Time for some breakfast." He coughed and looked to Rust. "Never let 'em dose you with whisky, son. Brings th' devil himself t' your dreams."

"You slept like a baby," Ma protested, the life coming back into her face at the strength in his voice.

"No wonder they wake up cryin' then!" Pa chuffed. "Comin' up with us, Maggie?" She nodded, and it was the three of them who set out with the telescope half an hour later.

"Be a scorcher tomorrow," Pa predicted as they made their way along the bank. He shook his head as they passed the Taylors' house. "Have t' have a word t' them about fires in weather like this. Lose th' whole valley in minutes."

"Mr Taylor told Dad last night they're going to sell. He said he thinks it's more for retired people. There's not enough for his son to do down here."

"Well, that's goin' t' break our hearts, isn't it, lass?" Pa chuckled. Then all at once he stopped, his face darkened in thought. Rust and Maggie stopped too, and waited. What was Pa puzzling over now?

"Still reckon it's th' sailors," he said at last, more to himself than to them. "Shouldn't really blame that Taylor feller."

"But I knocked the lamp off," Maggie said, half wanting the old man to blame her, even to be angry with her, rather than talk of ghosts again. "I was clumsy. I'd got a fright."

"There y' are, then," Pa exclaimed, "y' got a fright! They probably frightened y' so you would knock it off!" He reached out and gripped Rust's shoulder, the fingers biting into the soft muscle. "Dunno how I could ever have blamed you, son."

"But I didn't storm-tie her," Rust said quickly, snatching the chance to confess, wincing as his great-grandfather's fingers bit into his shoulder. "I thought I saw . . . something flying past across the bank and I panicked and—"

"Th' sailors!" Pa set his jaw and started forward again. "Weren't your fault."

Rust and Maggie looked at each other in despair.

At the old signal station Rust climbed the steps and straddled the wall, leaving Pa and Maggie with the telescope some four metres below. Although the tide had turned, it was still low enough for the high points of the Tambourine to be exposed. The surf beat up as the long swells, still just humps on either side, climbed the slope of the reef and broke about its teeth, the white fragments of torn water smoking back out to sea on the offshore breeze.

Rust scanned the long beach for some sign of the *Clinker*, and picked out instead the two black figures moving along it in the distance. Olly and Blue, he was sure. They'd said they would search and find her. He now felt certain that one of them—Bob, who'd driven to search the western beaches; Olly or Blue; or Pa, Maggie and himself—would find her. Then Pa would be free of the ghosts.

When he got home he'd tell Mom and Dad that Pa and Ma *shouldn't* come over to live. He'd tell his parents that they should persuade them to get heating and hot water now that the electricity was coming through. And perhaps Mom and Dad should spend the airfares Ma and Pa would have used to fly over and visit *them* in Australia.

He'd tell them it wasn't just Maggie they had as a friend here, but her father and mother as well. And he had to try to persuade Pa to let Bob and Anne lease some of the land. He wouldn't need to say forever—that would hurt Pa too much. Just to let them have some on a long lease.

He could imagine how pleased, even excited, Pa would be when he saw the land being used once more.

Rust thought of Maggie again. You couldn't really blame her for having been so—so *sour*. He would probably have been sour too, in her position. But she was great now.

Rust smiled to himself. Everything was going to be—

"There!" the old man's roar snapped Rust's eyes down to the scene directly below. Pa was standing back from the telescope and motioning to Maggie to put her eye to it.

"What?" Rust called to him.

"Come down an' have a look."

In his haste, Rust almost fell headlong down the old inner steps. He managed to regain his balance and emerged from the doorway, panting. "Put your eye on that," Pa said, mysteriously.

Maggie moved away and Rust took her place, allowing his eye to get adjusted to the telescope. She was there, the *Clinker* was there!—a dark shadow captured in the blue-green hump of water, now riding forward with the force moving through it, then dropping out behind and disappearing until the next swell.

"She doesn't seem to be even marked, Pa. She'll be all right!"

Pa's hand rested gently on Rust's shoulder. "Don't get your hopes up, son."

Rust pulled back from the eyepiece. "But I can get Olly and Blue and Bob and we can catch her before she comes on the rocks. *That* many of us can lift her out!"

"Not th' shore rocks goin' t' get her," Pa said. His face was drawn and his eyes strange again.

"But. . ." Rust peered into the telescope again. A smoke of white water rose from the sea. "I'll *swim* out!" he cried, jerking his eye away.

"No you won't, son. Too far an' too dangerous."

"But what are we going to *do*? Just stand here and watch her break up?"

"About all we *can* do, son." His jaws worked for a moment, his breath began to suck in and out. "Told y' what t' expect. Tambourine's claimin' 'er own."

"No," Rust whispered, looking again, aware of the heavy rasping breath close beside him. "No." Because then Pa would have reason to point to the ghosts of the dead sailors, reason to believe they would come back to claim everything else—everything else that was a part of the house but had come from the *Ohio*.

"Maggie!" he cried, lifting his head. He looked wildly about, up to the top of the wall, all around. She was gone.

"Always knew they'd come back f'r it all," Pa muttered, leaning back to look through the eyepiece.

Why had Maggie run off just when she was most needed? Pa might have listened to her.

"Pa, if I got Olly and Blue—" He didn't wait for an answer, but ran in through the door, climbed the steps and looked out. But they were so far away. He'd never get over to them and back and still have time to swim out, before. . . Rust turned his eyes back to the Tambourine, but was unable to make out the *Clinker* from here. Perhaps a shape in that swell, perhaps not. His hands gripped the stone till they hurt, his mind haunted by a vision of Pa in nights to come sitting, waiting for the ghosts, being the way he had been last night.

A flash from white water caught his eye. It was too far out to be a wave breaking, too close to be the teeth of the Tambourine. A fish splashing?

"Maggie!"

"Was'at?" Pa's voice was like a swishing blade from below.

"Maggie!" he shouted as he jumped up and clattered backwards down the steps, the word blatting from the walls against his own ears. "Maggie's going out to her, on her surfboard!"

"Damn girl! They'll 'ave 'er too."

"I'll go after her."

"Y' gotta," the old man agreed. "Get 'er back, son. Get 'er back afore they take 'er!"

Rust ran, wild leaping strides that carried him too fast to stop at the bottom, and he went over the sharp drop onto his hands and face, stunned for an instant. Then he scrambled to his feet and turned inland along the bank and up the tea-tree tunnel.

"Mrs Roberts, Mrs Roberts!" But he realized he didn't need her when he saw Bob's surfboard in the lean-to.

"Rust?"

"Maggie's gone out to the Tambourine!" he cried back without waiting.

Pa was near the bottom of the track from the old signal station. "Hurry, son!" he urged wildly.

Rust sprinted along the cliff beach and across the new bar, not waiting to take off his sneakers, the first wave lifting and throwing him back. *Slow down*, he told himself.

He waited for a few seconds before rolling under the break with the board on top of him. He came up on the other side and dropped onto the board full-length to lunge back with his arms spread wide, driving the board up the next wave before its crest chipped. The next one was easy, and after that nothing but humps that barely even slowed him.

Maggie! He grinned and got to his knees, balanced himself and straightened up. She must be there already: white water was spraying up in a way that it wouldn't from the reef. Bailing?

He dropped down and stroked again, pacing himself now, conserving his strength for the bailing. She was saving the *Clinker*, and that meant she had saved Pa, and Ma — saved them from so much distress that he could not really even begin to imagine it.

"You should have told me you were going," he spluttered as he reached her.

"He would have stopped us."

He grabbed the gunwale and tipped himself in over the side, glancing to see where her board was and noticing that she had tethered it by the leg-rope to the *Clinker* and left it floating.

"Hurry," she gasped. "Help me, we're nearly on it."

He looked up, shocked when a black tooth stabbed up

through the surface just ahead. He hadn't realized they were so close.

"Can't we tow her away?"

"Not full of water," she panted. "I tried. Wouldn't even move. Like she's being pulled. . ."

He rolled in and tied the end of his board's leg-rope next to Maggie's, then stood and started to scoop with cupped hands.

"She's rising, she's rising!" Maggie cried.

Again a tooth of the reef punctured the water ahead, throwing a spit of white foam into the wind — like a rabid dog, Rust thought with sudden horror as the water flew over the side from his hands. She wasn't going to be buoyant enough to tow before the black teeth sank into her.

"Hurry," Maggie begged, almost exhausted. "If she goes down he'll *die*."

Rust stopped bailing and looked out. The reef rose black and green from the depths, a great razorback ridge of the sea floor. He climbed over the side.

"Get back in!" Maggie yelled desperately.

He jammed his feet against something solid, slipped from it, jammed again and leaned against the gunwale. "Bail!" he said. "I can hold her off till you get her high. We can do it, Maggie, we can!"

She paused, just for a moment, and the slow smile he had first seen on her mother's face melted through the fear that had clung to hers, and she began to bail again, more slowly now, slowly and steadily.

"He won't have to fear the ghosts any more," she said, softly.

Rust felt the solidness of the rock beneath his soles, the *realness* of it. Nothing fearsome. Nothing malevolent. Just rock, solid Earth rock.

"And when I'm gone you'll look after him again."

"Yes," she whispered. "Yes. And. . . I'm glad you came."